D0407901

BREAKOUT

PAUL FLEISCHMAN

Cricket Books

A Marcato Book

Chicago

For *Marc Aronson*

The car coughed all the way down the freeway entrance, gargled raucously with each change of gear, then shivered like a fever patient when Del tried to take it above sixty. The seat springs were shot, leaving her butt below sea level and her knees in the clouds. The right outside mirror had been lost somewhere on life's journey. The wheels pulled strongly to the left. An otherworldly whine issued from the air vents. The "Service Engine Soon" light flickered on, then went out—a messenger shot in the back. It was an '83 Datsun, born before CD players, power locks, air bags. On the plus side, the worn leather steering-wheel cover felt homey. And the car was hers.

She let out a scream of joy. The mother of two in the Volvo beside her gave her a glance and slid over two lanes. Del could barely believe everything had gone smoothly. In her mind she played the breakout scene from *Armed and Dangerous,* the old black-and-white prison movie they'd had at the house in Glendale: Mack plumping up the dummy on his bed, Slim lifting the floorboards to reveal the tunnel, then Jake, the leader, checking his watch, nodding to the others, and muttering, "I been waitin' for this a long time." She said the words aloud in his Brooklyn accent, saw him wiping his forehead and spitting on the floor, then gave the car more gas and shouted out his next line: "Let's bust outta this pukehole!" She drew the line out, then uncorked it again even louder, and again, then a fourth time, spraying it like champagne at the cars around her, at the schoolgirls on the overpass, at the man collecting litter, at the yellow city bus, at the beaming couple on the billboard, at the palm trees and the skyscrapers and the hills in the distance—at all of L.A.

It was July and already hot at eight-fifteen. For three days a Santa Ana wind had been blowing, a furnace door left open. The heat turned up the volume on all her feelings: jubilation, fear, and an eerie sense of weightlessness, as if she were an astronaut free-floating in space—one who's just cut her own cord.

She stole a glance at the temperature controls but couldn't find the air-conditioning switch. With her eyes on the road, she sent her right hand clambering blindly over the console like an elephant trunk, starting the rear wiper, the rear defrost, the warning lights. Then it came to her that the ponytailed seller had grinned when he'd drawled "externally sourced" in reply to her question about A/C. She'd bought his answer without comment at the time. Suddenly, his meaning was clear. She grabbed the wobbly handle and rolled down the window.

"Jerk," she snapped.

Tilting her head, she bathed in the air flow, trying to wash out the knowledge that her inexperience had been so visible. She felt as if she'd walked down Wilshire in her underwear. Could everybody see that she was barely seventeen, desperate, and didn't know brake fluid from fudge syrup? "Farther down the line," she warned the man out loud, her standard karmic threat. Then she remembered. He was part of the past. He'd sold the car to Del. But Del was done with. She was Elena now. Elena Franco.

She needed music, turned on the radio, and hunted for KLOS. A red Miata blared at her. She'd drifted out of her lane. She jumped back to the right, approached the San Diego Freeway, and repeated her route out loud: "Santa Monica Freeway *east*. Follow signs for *Interstate 10*. Ten all the way to Phoenix. Then north on whatever-it-is." Then she added, "And no mess-ups." Then, "Piece of cake." She felt for the map, making sure it was there on the passenger seat underneath her stuffed collie. "And Lassie knows the way," she added. Del gave the dog a pat. She imagined herself leaving the gray part of the map and entering the olive, then the dark green, could taste the coolness in the air there, revivifying as a waterfall. She looked at the tree-shaped air freshener, formerly pine-scented, formerly bright green, that had come with the car at no extra charge.

"Gonna take you back home," she promised it. "Back to the mountains."

From out of nowhere, in a split-second shiver, she sensed that her mother was somewhere in L.A. Then the thought was behind her, like a car speeding past.

"Elena?"

"That's me."

"I'm Carla. Here for the interview. Sorry I'm late. I'll be quick."

"That's good, 'cause the curtain goes up in forty-five minutes and I need half an hour all alone first. Hope you don't mind me doing my makeup. What's the name of your paper?"

"Kaleidoscope. Arts and events with a little muckraking on the side. OK if I record us?"

"Go for it. Just be sure to take the 'ums' out of my quotes. And no fragments or run-ons, you know? Make it read like English. And be sure to describe the dressing room as 'opulent' and crammed with bouquets. Just kidding."

"OK. Recording. The play's called Breakout. A one-woman show, written and performed by Elena Franco. And this is the Denver premiere, right?"

"Denver, North America, the universe. This is it. All zeroes on the odometer."

"Wow. Are you nervous?"

"Thanks for reminding me. Of course I'm nervous! I hate rejection, in all its forms. Especially in the form of people not attending my plays, taking phone calls while they're attending my plays, and letting their seats bang when they leave in the middle of my plays."

"From what the theater faxed me, the show's about a traffic jam in Los Angeles. Is that where you live?"

"I did till high school, but I'm in Boulder now."

"How old are you?"

"Twenty-five. Could you hand me that mascara?"

"How many plays have you written?"

"This is number nine. The third one I've gotten produced. Now if I could only get a few reviews."

"I'll be doing that."

"Cool. And what form of payment do you prefer when being bribed?"

"One of those Hershey kisses would probably do the job."

"Here, take twenty."

"So apparently there's a lot about cars in the play. Are you into cars?"

"Into cars? I hate cars. The first one I owned was this ancient Datsun that had an asthma attack every time it went uphill. So of course I took it to the mountains, and I eventually ended up working at this motel in Taos, where of course it died on me in a couple of weeks. My initiation into the wonderful world of automobiles. They're like kids, only more expensive. You gotta bathe 'em and buy 'em stuff and take 'em to the emergency room and worry about people stealing 'em. I've already got a child for all that. A daughter who's my one and only and tells me I'm hers. No car ever said that to me."

"Are you married?"

"Single. Probably because I'm insanely picky about who I'd let help raise my girl. And I'm probably too much of a control freak for anyone to put up with anyway."

"Yeah?"

"Yeah. I write all my own copy for theater programs and try to edit everyone else's. I boss the lighting and set people around. I really like getting what I want, you know? When I wanted a baby, I got myself pregnant. With boyfriends, I'm always getting in trouble telling 'em where to park and what to order in restaurants. You're not going to print this, right?"

"So are any of the characters in the show based on you?"

"Any of 'em? All of 'em!"

"It's autobiography?"

"It's fiction. Meaning autobiography seen through weird, wavy glass. I mean, I'm not comically helpless like the new father in the show, and I sure don't drive a Lincoln Continental, but I know about trying to mix work and parenting, what it's like when I'm trying to type with one hand and hold a thermometer in my daughter's mouth with the other."

"So where did this bunch of characters come from? From a certain time in your life?"

"Funny you should ask. I think I'll leave that one alone. What do you think of the earrings? Too big? They look like freaking wind chimes."

"I like 'em."

"Yeah?"

"Yeah."

"OK. They're in. Anyway. Back to your question. A partial answer. The play mainly comes from when I was younger. But all that stuff's seen through my eyes now, with everything that's happened since, especially this breakthrough I had a year ago. It's like those paintings

Monet did of the same haystack at different times. The hay's yellow in one, then orange, then purple. You keep getting older and changing, and the scenes you look back on change because of that. I was pretty angry and impossible in high school. But in the show there's an argument between a parent and a teenager, and when I was writing it, suddenly it hit me that I was siding with the mother now and making fun of my old impossible self. You can't step into the same river twice. Or the same memory, you know?"

"So why a traffic jam? It seems like such a strange subject to pick."

"That was part of the lure. A misshapen, unwanted subject that actually had a lot going for it. And in L.A. it's not strange—it's daily life. One summer I was in a killer jam like this one. The kind you never forget. The play's sort of based on that, and on issues from back then that I'm still working on. But altered, disguised, given to different characters. Changed. From life into art. Like in the play, I changed the jam to winter, to keep the drivers in their cars longer, so I could get into their little worlds and build up to the scene when they finally get out and start interacting with each other. That's what writers do."

"Do you think you'll ever do the show in L.A.?"

"Man, what are you, a massage therapist? You know just where it hurts. Short answer: No. Off-the-record answer, just for you: The things I tell about myself in the show are all true, except that I don't actually have an

agent in L.A.—or any agent, period—and I didn't fly
out there last year. I've never actually gone back since I
left. And never wanted to. So, no. It's not a place I'd be
comfortable performing. End of interview, OK? Whew.
That got my mind off the jitters. So tell me, was anybody
milling around on the sidewalk? The first play I ever did,
the theater sat eighty, two people showed up. And they sat
on opposite sides. Two bowling pins. I swear I went
cross-eyed. One laughed, the other didn't. To bring in a
crowd, theaters should hire people to mill around on the
sidewalk, don't you think? Like duck decoys. It works
with birds, right? Whoa. It's seven-thirty. Get me a copy
of the story, OK? Sorry to shoo you out."

    "Break a leg."

    "How 'bout 'axle.'"

    "Cute."

    "Could you say it? For luck?"

    "Break an axle."

    "Thanks."

 Traffic thickened past the San Diego interchange. Cars closed in around Del as if they were all being herded into a pen, other drivers now visible in unasked-for detail. She watched smoke uncoiling like Arabic calligraphy from the cigarette held by the man

9

in front, and through his windows she looked one car farther, where two unbelted toddlers flailed at each other in Punch and Judy fashion. Del smiled inside, hoarding her secret, savoring how little the others could see of her.

They knew nothing of her long swims behind the waves, the joy of diving into a new medium, becoming a new creature, leaving behind the rules and ranting of Opal Pewitt—a loony from Lubbock and her current foster mother. They were unaware of the string of deposits from her video-store job that had bought her the car. They hadn't seen her park it a half-mile from her house, visiting at night to drop off thrift-shop clothes, groceries, the tent. They would have laughed to see her disguised just an hour before, in baggy sweats and huge sunglasses and floppy hat, walking with a quirky gait picked up from a passerby, unfolding her Little Mermaid towel on the sand at her spot south of Venice Pier, quickly arranging her sandals and sunscreen, discreetly dropping her bathing cap in the water. Then to the gas station bathroom to change clothes and cut off her hair. Then to the car, and onto the freeway.

She flicked the air freshener, sending it spinning, and congratulated herself on her brilliance. If none of her other job ideas panned out, she could always write a book: Faking Your Own Death for Dummies.

She took off her cap and felt her head in wonder. Minutes before, her hair had been a steamy, wriggling mass of curls, heavy as an armload of seaweed. Over the years, it had firmly resisted straightening, mousse, braiding, cornrows, and everything L'Oréal could throw at it. Now it was half an inch long. Her head felt light as a balloon. She sat tall, glanced in the mirror, and barely recognized herself. A good sign. She'd work on the uneven patches that night. Maybe she'd actually come to like it. There was nothing like simulating your death to spur action on chronic hair problems. The other advantages over mere running away were just as appealing: No search for her. No being returned to Opal. No being placed with someone else even worse or in some zoo of a group home. An end to the Ferris wheel of social workers, therapists, lawyers, advocates, to assessments and interviews and reports and recommendations. An end to her file—Tolstoy-thick, battered and brown-edged with thumbing. A life without a file, just like other people! No state inspector peering into her tent. No eight other pairs of hands helping her raise it. Not a boring class in Independent Living Skills, like the one she'd just taken, but real independence! Actual living! Why wait another year till graduation? She was ready to start living her life right now. But not a sequel to her old one. A new life. Bare wood. Blank page.

She wondered if her death would be in the news. She wasn't scheduled to show up at work until three, and Opal wouldn't be home before six. If it made the news at all, it wouldn't be for a day. The bathing cap was meant to suggest drowning, but sharks might take the rap. She'd hoped to tiptoe out quietly enough not to wake the media. Then again, reading about your own memorial service would be cool—yet another advantage of faking your death over actually dying. With an industrial-strength disguise, you could even attend it. Del pictured the scene.

"Who's the Eskimo woman in the furs with the caribou-skin sun mask?"

"Said she was one of Del's caseworkers."

She imagined the crowd in the chapel: the few foster parents who hadn't rejoiced to hear she'd died, one or two social workers, her neighbor from the El Monte house. She listened in on their conversations: the Dodgers, traffic, work. Disappointing but probably true. Then she added her chemistry teacher to the scene, Mr. Kielbohn, popularly known as Mr. Carbon. He was wearing his tweed vest and bow tie, the only teacher who'd likely show up. She approached him. Through the mouth slit in her mask she whispered into his ear, "Do not worry. The seal spirit told me she very happy now where she is. Del love water very much."

To which he replied, "Just a *heck* of a substance. Let me show you something about water. . . ."

Del returned to the present and felt suddenly uneasy to realize she was leaving the Pacific behind. It would seem strange not to have that geographical anchor. Or anything else familiar around her. She hated L.A., but it was all she'd known. She'd twice lived within earshot of a freeway and gotten used to falling asleep to the sound. Would they have Winchell's Donuts and California rolls in Arizona? The prospect of so much newness was frightening, the dose too concentrated. A road sign advanced toward her: "Downtown Los Angeles." She had no idea what she'd find on the other side. For an instant, she wished she could turn around, then gripped the wheel tighter and steered toward the east.

Los Angeles! City of tanned shoulders! Smog-spewing, pay-per-viewing, sitcom maker for the world! Mall builder! Pierced-tongue purveyor of tacos! Surfboard toter, deal closer, looter, shooter, barbecuer, black-jacketed valet parker of a million BMWs! City of thronged roads! Drive-through city! City whose dwellers see the sun through sunroofs, its rays pouring through like revelation

and tanning the youthful, muscled, tattooed, sunscreened shoulders of Los Angeles!

Probably half the people in this theater moved here from there, right? You know what I'm talking about. L.A. Home of drive-in movies. Also drive-through burgers, bagels, banking, booze. Not to mention drive-in church. And why not? What is sitting in church like? Gridlock, without the bucket seats. In both cases, a good time to clean under your nails. A chance for profound examination of your behavior: "Why didn't I wait until rush hour was over?" Staring at the head in front of you, wondering if she did her hair by sticking it out the window at the car wash. Wondering if God meant you to wear bangs. Wondering when we can all go home.

Roads and revelation go together. Saint Paul had his vision on the road to Damascus. Blinded him. Knocked him flat on the ground.

Mine came on a road, too, in my twenty-fourth year. In L.A., on the San Diego Freeway. Northbound, near the Mulholland exit. A metaphysical, out-of-body, out-of-automobile experience. A Scenic Vista vision of Los Angeles, of the whole freeway of life.

Could we dim the lights just a little? Thanks.

Wow. Weird. That's exactly how it started with Saint Paul. He looked up and saw light. A blazing light from heaven. Struck him blind for three days.

Mine wasn't the three-day variety. It's been more than a year and it's still with me, still revealing itself, a flower in the mind, endlessly unfolding, a new petal every day.

Mine also started with light. Or rather, lights. Red lights. Thousands and thousands of them.

 A mustached motorcyclist drew even with Del, taking a break from watching traffic to check her out in detail. She was tall and looked older than her age. She felt his eyes on her and didn't feel flattered. Just call me Creepbait, she thought. She sped up slightly, causing the Datsun to tremble, and imagined a new warning light coming on: "High Speeds Make Car Very Nervous." Then "Car Has Had Extremely Hard Life." He pulled even again.

"Go, Falcons!" he yelled, grinning at her.

She had no idea what he meant but rolled up her window on general principle. This sent him roaring off between lanes. She watched him disappear like a thread pulled out of fabric, then thought to take a look at her cap. Above a wide-winged black bird were the words "Atlanta Falcons." She hadn't paid attention to this when she'd bought it, looking only for something to cover her clipped head, something no one would associate with her. Del loathed team sports. Then she remembered: That was her old self. She needed to start living the part she was dressed for, her interim identity, until she began building a permanent replacement. She plopped the cap back in place. "Go, Falcons," she said. Then a second time, from the pit of her stomach, as a believer who had the team logo on underwear, mouse pad, and gravestone: "Go, *Fal-cons!*" She wondered what sport it was they played.

She cranked her window back down and considered the rest of her wardrobe. To avoid suspicion of running away, she'd had to leave everything behind—her boombox, CDs, her new Doc Martens, her lava lamp, and all her clothes. She viewed her Yale T-shirt and rolled her eyes. She'd bought it and the cap and her shorts at the same thrift shop, not thinking about the psychological ensemble. Great, she thought. I'm a Georgia redneck *and* a snooty Ivy Leaguer. She fingered the Hang Ten logo on her shorts. "*And* a freaking beach bunny," she said out loud. The shirt was gray, the shorts hot pink, colors she never wore, chosen for that reason. It would be an interesting experiment. Clothes should be a comfort, but these grated on her eyes and created a constant, low-level unease.

Then again, she'd always felt slightly out of place in her own skin.

The Robertson exit came and went. Speed-reading all the road signs, Del grasped for confirmation that she was still on 10 East, like a ninety-year-old clutching a banister. A garbage truck passed her on the right.

"Where's your pride?" she chided her car. "You gonna let that hulk pass you?" On the other hand, better to have it past her and gone than in her mirror for miles. Garbage trucks always made her hands sweat, taking her back to her fourth foster home. As her file didn't say where she'd been found as a newborn, that family's son had taunted her with being a Dumpster baby, a charge with many consequences: her knocking out two of his teeth, a request for her removal from the home, nightmares in which she was devoured by garbage trucks, and a desperate interest in perfume, itself the spur to her shoplifting career. She breathed in the scent she'd put on that morning— not foreign, like her clothes, but her usual Chanel. It was nicotine for the nose, a soother she wasn't ready to leave behind.

Cars exchanged lanes as if braiding a Maypole. Del gained on the garbage truck against her will and felt the sweat push through her pores. Eight years old, arriving in her fifth home, she knew she needed to fill the vacuum surrounding her origins, and did so, supplying so much invented information about her lawyer mother and fireman father and her birth in room 311 of Los Angeles Hospital that tormentors looked for other points of entry. In actuality, having no knowledge about her parents, the doctors at the time had put her on a respiratory monitor in case she was a crack baby and had watched as well for fetal alcohol syndrome, facts that entered her file and shrieked at anyone interested in adopting her. Others were put off by her mélange of features: light brown skin, wide nose, thick lips, eyes and cheekbones that might have been Vietnamese or Guatemalan, curly hair the color of Georgia clay. She was too black to be white and too white to be black. And then, after a time, she was simply too old. "They all want to adopt 'em brand new," she'd overheard her fourth caseworker telling her fifth foster father. She'd nearly been adopted by her foster parents when she was six, until the mother became pregnant with twins; Del's room was needed and she was passed on to her next family. She'd never felt connected or committed to her foster parents' worlds, just as they hadn't committed to her. This fueled the discipline problems that sped her passage through their homes. "Once they hit three, they never get out," the caseworker had said. Del heard those words now, saw the woman's cheerless face, and addressed her aloud: "*I'm* getting out." She reached and rolled down the passenger window, welcomed in the rushing air, and shouted her sixth mother's favorite phrase: "I'm a *gone* pec*an*," the last two words rhyming. She burst into a laugh, glorying in her escape.

Then she saw traffic stopped ahead.

I went out to L.A. a year ago to do a play of mine at the most microscopic, dingiest, hardest-to-park-at theater with the most warbly phone message and highest number of safety violations that my agent could find. He's supposed to have lots of Hollywood connections. He'd said to expect some bigwigs in the audience. The theater was near the harbor in San Pedro in an old fish-packing plant, a long flight up a metal staircase that Spiderman would have broken his neck on. No advertising. Rat turds in the dressing room. You could hear the backstage toilet running all night. Plus, the place smelled like halibut. When I asked all the Hollywood producers and directors to raise their hands—nothing. Despite which, to reward my agent for this, I was actually driving to North Hollywood that Monday, after the run, to show him some of my new material, so he could quick e-mail his extensive contacts in Tierra del Fuego and probably book me for Penguinfest.

My route was up the San Diego Freeway, then over on the Ventura. Every freeway has its own personality, like a wine. "Capricious, mildly psychotic, with hints of broken glass and a long, smoggy finish." After eight years living in Taos and Boulder, the San Diego felt so big—a huge, new school where everything's strange. It's maybe eight-thirty in the morning, traffic is actually moving, amazingly, and I'm almost there, past Westwood, climbing through the Santa Monica Mountains toward the Valley. The radio's on, but I'm not really listening. I'm eyeing the guy in front of me who's got this big, irregular bald spot that looks oddly like the state of Montana. I mean exactly like it. I can practically see the skiers on the mountains. I'm debating: baldness or recent brain surgery? Then I notice that the Doors are playing on the radio and the song is "People Are Strange." Ain't it the truth. The guy's having trouble staying in his lane. I'm thinking lobotomy. And with the way the insurance companies work, he'd probably had the surgery an hour ago and was driving himself home with a catheter draining into his coffee thermos.

I need a break from his problems. I look to my left. A woman driving a Beetle is peering into the mirror and plucking her eyebrows one-handed. Nothing unusual there. Then I look to the right, and do a double take. There's a gray-bearded man in an old Cadillac and he's actually playing a French horn while he drives. This is new. I grew up in California. I'd seen a trumpet before. Harmonicas. A ukulele at a red light. But this is my first French horn. And just as I'm thinking they should rename it the Jim Morrison Memorial Freeway, all of a sudden, in a wave, in parade, row after row of red lights come toward me, a message speeding down the freeway's spinal column. And the message is: Stop.

We stop. We sit. We wait. We pray for deliverance.

After five minutes, I notice the first engine being turned off. This action spreads, unevenly, the way house lights come on at dusk. I look at my watch. My agent's expecting me in fifteen minutes. Then I need to drive back to LAX, turn in my rental car, and pray I make my eleven-thirty flight. I drum my fingers on the wheel like everyone else. I look around. I see sighing, swearing, cell phones, frantic searching for relaxation tapes. You can feel a thousand plans melting like snowflakes in a thousand palms.

I turn off my engine. I open my sunroof. It's February and cold for L.A. The freeway is what it never is: quiet . . . and still. It's gone from a liquid to a solid. Our cars are locked together in the closest possible configuration. We're atoms in a crystal. And we're not going anywhere soon.

In L.A., immobility is not next to godliness. It's next to failure, stagnation, death. Every year, every student in Los Angeles is bused to the La Brea tarpits to see what happened to the mammoths who got stuck in the tar.

"They stopped moving and died!" scream the teachers. "Don't let it happen to you!"

The same thought goes through all our heads: We're not moving, the way God intended us to! It's too horrible. We might as well be plants! Marooned forever with the collection of kooks that fate has placed around us. The woman on my left is still plucking her eyebrows. The French horn player is now behind me. Lobotomy's still in front. To my right there's a blond flipping magazine pages as if she's under the dryer at the beauty parlor. I feel like I'm in Fellini's 8½—that opening scene in the traffic jam, all the drivers with those bizarre faces, all trapped in their cars, staring at each other.

And then something weird begins. I feel myself growing strangely light. Helium instead of oxygen inside me. Lighter than air. Powerfully buoyant, straining upward. I don't know what's happening. Suddenly, I hear my seat belt unlatching. It falls away. And slowly, astoundingly, I begin rising up from my seat—and float out my sunroof. Up, miraculously, into the air, just like the man in 8½ who floats out of his car. I can't believe it. No one around me seems to notice. No pointing or whipping out video cameras. It dawns on me: I must be invisible. I move higher, slowly, astonished and delighted, unafraid, arms at my sides, hearing my dress rippling like a sail, falling upward through the bracing air, up through the canyon's shade *and into the bright light above, able finally to look down on all the miles of cars below, able, I realize, to see into them, and, more amazing still, to see into the lives of their drivers, able to behold the whole scene at once, watching in wonderment as it unfolds.*

"I don't need this!" Del yelled at the wall of cars stopped in front of her. Then, again, louder. Then, "Come on, goddammit!" Her windows were down, but she didn't care; everyone else's were up, to keep in their air-conditioned air. She banged twice on her steering wheel. She knew she wasn't acting like April's Student of the Month, which she'd been. Then again, deportment had never been her strong suit. Suddenly she noticed there were no cars in the oncoming lanes. Her eyes expanded. Something was very wrong. She leaned back, exhaled, and switched to pleading with the Fates: "Come on! *Please!*"

In front of her an SUV with tinted windows blocked her vision. One lane to the right, the garbage truck, now two cars ahead, did the same. "Jerks," Del addressed them both. She stuck her head out her window, then grabbed hold of the doorframe, hoisted her upper body up and out—and nearly buckled in disbelief. Lines of cars stretched to the limit of sight, as if the scene were a study in perspective.

"Jesus Christ," she murmured. The view knocked the wind out of her. She locked her elbows, unable to stop looking. The prospect was as static as a graduation class photo, the subjects pressed into lanes instead of bleachers, a moment in the freeway's life frozen for posterity. She had a *Twilight Zone* sensation, imagining the cars empty, the drivers long dead and decomposed. Class of 1908. Then her eye returned her to the present, snagged by the sole movement to be seen: two helicopters hovering in the far distance, tiny as gnats.

She collapsed back into her seat. "You gotta be kidding," she muttered. Her hands flapped aimlessly up to the wheel, then alit on her knees, then scratched her scalp. To her left, a man in a Lexus unrolled a silver sun guard in front of his windshield, reclined his seat all the way back, and slipped on an eye mask, settling in for a siege. In front of her, the SUV's brake lights went out. Needing to save gas, Del turned off her own engine. Then she yanked the key out of the ignition, strangled it in her fist, and finally flung it down.

"I can't believe this!" she screamed. Then the tears came. The day she tries to escape, her route's

blocked. The *one time* she finally takes control of her life, it's snatched away. The world was against her. As if that were news. It didn't want her to succeed. It couldn't stand her to be happy. It hated that her saving and planning and pretending had gone exactly as she'd hoped. She bent to pick up the key, bumped her head on the wheel, slugged it back, and jammed the key in the ignition. She stuck her head back out the window, praying that she'd see traffic moving. It wasn't.

She clenched her teeth, shut her eyes, then imagined gunning her Datsun and plowing every car in its path off the freeway. She then saw herself breezing down an empty highway, flying past the "Welcome to Arizona" sign. She put her hands on the wheel, as if to persuade reality to comply. When it didn't, she found herself in a *King Kong* remake in which she ran up to the accident, picked up the wrecked cars, and hurled them off the freeway. This was followed by the empty highway happy ending. She knew she was being childish but couldn't help it. The lack of motion was killing her. She felt stuck in a freeze frame. She reclined her seat, shooting suddenly back, grabbed her collie, and buried her face in it.

I look down at the cars, strung out for miles in both directions, two ribbons joined in the center by a big, messy bow. It's a video on Pause. A painting: Still Life with Twenty Thousand Cars. I can see into all of them at once.

Fifty-four percent of the drivers are still staring ahead, hands on the wheel, the way people keep looking at a TV screen after it's been turned off. Eighteen percent still have their engines going, running the heat or refusing to face facts. Twelve percent are having Houdini fantasies: throwing off the steel chains, opening the chest, bursting free. One of these opens the door of his hulking Yukon SUV and jumps down.

He's large, blond, in jeans and work boots. He's only been stopped for nine and a half minutes, but he's twitchy with coffee and wild with boredom. He stares up the freeway like a sheriff in a showdown. Around him, other drivers start to take notice. Hope surges inside some of them. Maybe he knows something. Maybe he can do the impossible. Rambo has arrived.

He throws down his cigarette and grinds it flat. He aims his remote at his car and fires. His SUV blares, sending two separate Chihuahuas into cardiac arrest. Still holding the remote, he looks around, his gaze saying, You mess with my Yukon, I've got a few other buttons on this thing just for you. An animator in a Camry picks up an antiviolence worksheet from his son's school and starts sketching a remote that shoots thirty-foot flames. Rambo

pockets his. Then he marches off. Necks stretch to watch.
He's all there is to look at, the only channel on TV. In
their minds, several drivers see him dragging a fallen
eighteen-wheeler off the road, single-handedly clearing the
logjam. One pictures him bending back a section of
guardrail. Another sees him performing surgery in the bed
of a pickup. Scoffers include a marriage and family coun-
selor who thinks, "How'd you like to be married to
that?" A recording engineer follows his progress, snidely
humming "Hit the Road, Jack." Four cars to the rear, a
retired second-grade teacher in a creaky Chevrolet Impala
shakes her head, thinks back to the class of 1971, and
says out loud, "Can't sit still, just like Cecil Weingartner,"
then watches him disappear around a bend.

 Del squeezed her eyes shut and took command of her
mental life by plunging into the ocean, an antidote to
the heat and captivity. It was early morning in her
mind, and she was moving north behind the waves,
swimming with eyes closed, as she sometimes did,
giving herself entirely to the water, rising and falling
with its respirations. It had been the only good thing
about living in Venice. She'd hated the school and
hated Opal. The woman's air-raid siren of a voice
couldn't reach her behind the waves. All Del sometimes heard from her life on land were the gospel

songs from the house in El Monte, the rapturous accounts of the tranquility awaiting "on the other shore," a realm she'd felt she'd found in the ocean. The pounding waves were no more than a muffled heartbeat on this side, the ear-opening quiet a constant surprise. She felt the water flowing over and through her, felt herself dissolving in it, imagined herself invisible to the Coast Guard planes that passed.

Del moved into the back seat to avoid the sun. She drank from her water bottle, squirted her head, then opened her ice chest and dipped a bandana into the arctic water at the bottom. She leaned back onto her winter clothes and laid the wet cloth over her eyes. She unpaused her fantasy. She swam for a while, then pictured herself walking out of the ocean, spent, salty, skin tingling, and falling into another realm: her beach towel. She stretched out upon it, facedown, eyes closed. Her tongue licked at the salt on her lips. Inside her, the motion from swimming unwound like a clock running down. She lay in a daze, sucking up the towel's stored warmth through her pores. She could feel its familiar nap against her cheek, and suddenly the scene from *8½* began playing in her head, her favorite in the movie: the man flashing back to when he was a boy, bathing in a vat of wine with other children, then being lifted into a vast, white towel held by his adoring mother, who wraps him up, carries him up the long stairway to his room, tucking him into the white sheets of his bed on a summer night, bending over him, kissing him, telling him he's the sweetest boy in all the world. It was the house in Glendale where there'd been the big movie collection and a TV/VCR in her room. She'd been about the same age as the boy. She'd rewound the scene time after time, had badgered her foster parents with requests to be dried, forming a fierce attachment to their one white towel, which she stole when she left. She'd studied her face for Italian features, wondering if she might have relatives in Italy who had such a bed, empty and waiting, who'd vie for the right to be the last to kiss her good night. She'd begun speaking nonsense Italian, duplicating the sound and squabbling-sparrows rhythm—and so her career as a mimic began.

She'd always had a knack for imitation and of necessity was unusually observant. This was vital for discerning the natural laws of each new home, the moods and likes and limits of her caretakers. Now she began not simply taking in information about others, but dressing up in it. She no longer had been born in Los Angeles Hospital, but in Rome—"Roma," as she corrected all who mispronounced it. Until her foster parents packed them away, she watched every Italian film in the house, picking up common words and phrases, choosing a family for herself from their casts: her mother from *8 1/2*, her father the tightrope-walker from *La Strada*, her uncles and aunts and grandparents and cousins from *Amarcord* and *Cinema Paradiso* and *The Bicycle Thief*. She regaled teachers, classmates, therapists, and telemarketers with tales of traveling circuses and visits to spas and bathing in wine, rendering her extended, eccentric family in posture, gestures, manner of speech. For fear of encouraging her, her foster mother stopped serving spaghetti.

Few of Del's listeners were taken in. She grew furious when they mocked her or tried to reason her out of her claims. After a year, she left Italy and entered the world of books. She submerged herself in the Little House on the Prairie series, followed by the Narnia books, Tolkien, several years of science fiction, then Dickens, Thomas Hardy, then Russian novels, imagining herself dwelling in those worlds, squeezing herself onto the family trees, changing her name from Audelia to Audrey or Anya Petrovna as required. She shared this shape-shifting with no one. Sometimes, though, she entertained her foster siblings with impersonations of foster parents—accents, walks, smoking mannerisms—to her audience's delight. At other times, she put herself into the skins of strangers, borrowing their gestures, imagining their lives, taking them out for a test drive. Arriving at a department store as herself, she would leave as the married Brit at the perfume counter, flaunting her north of England accent, walking the way married women walk, shopping in a men's store for her imaginary husband, then discarding that life two stores down the mall in favor of a Jamaican cashier's. She sat up now, looked down a side street, glimpsed a UPS truck turning a corner, and felt ready to give up a limb for the right to switch places with the driver for real.

She wiped her face with the bandana, then rolled down the rear windows and listened. There was no sound of sirens, tow trucks, hope.

"Christ on a goddamn freaking crutch!" she yelled, a modification of her seventh foster father's pet phrase. No one around her reacted to this. Half of them seemed to be gabbing on cell phones. She might have been alone in the desert. As if testing an echo, she yelled it again, louder. She had a vision of Jesus hobbling by on crutches, leaving the Porsches and Corvettes in his dust.

She looked down at her collie doll. "Come on, Lassie!" she snapped. *"Do something!"* She held him in front of her face, then threw him at the windshield, slapping the air freshener. She watched its demon-possessed dance and thought, You are the most pathetic tree I've ever seen. Faded to a pale green, it jerked about, dropping bits of foam. You've definitely been in L.A. too long, she told it silently. We both gotta get to the mountains.

She imagined it yelling back at her: Mountains? Are you crazy? I live in a car! I'll die up there!

Del turned away, then pictured Opal shrieking at her. How the woman would have loved the chance, since she seemed to have spent a lifetime watching the Paranoia Channel, seeing pregnancy lurking in every boy's phone call and date-rape potions in every soft drink. Del counted her the most inept of her foster parents and was amazed she'd been licensed to keep an ant farm much less kids. *"Arizona?"* she imagined Opal yell. "Are you *crazy?"* She could hear the woman screaming to her about rattlesnakes, heat-stroke, vampire bats, and checking her bra for scorpions before putting it on. She snorted at this aural mirage. With another part of her brain, however, she wondered if she was likely to meet up with any of those dangers. Her stomach felt suddenly unsteady. She'd never been to Arizona, didn't really know what she was getting into, had only the tiniest experience camping. For an instant, it seemed as if she were repeating her mother's act of abandonment with herself, leaving herself among strangers—hikers, prospectors, rain-dancing Indians—this time amid forests instead of city streets. She wondered if she carried the abandonment gene. Avoiding the thought, she glanced up at the tree.

Neither of us knows zip about nature! it said.

"We'll worry about that later," Del replied out loud.

Cell phones are ringing all down the freeway. I identify forty-eight different rings. They trill and twitter like bird calls. Then behind all that, my ear catches something different. The sounds of the rattle and the drum. Ancient sounds, rising once again from the Santa Monica Mountains. I look down. They're not coming from a shaman's hut. Instead, I trace them to the plush, black-leather interior of a Lincoln Continental. In the car, an eleven-month-old baby and her father, one shaking her pink plastic rattle, the other drumming his thick fingers on the dash. The morning is not going as planned.

His wife left the afternoon before for five days, off to Tucson to see her mother through heart surgery. It's the first time she's left her husband alone with Brittany, their only child. She had serious qualms about this, as if she were abandoning their daughter to a stranger. Before she left, she made him five complete dinners, labeled them, and arranged them at eye level in the freezer. She filled the cupboard with jars of baby food. She packed. Then came the afterthoughts.

Her husband was something of a stranger to the kitchen. She took the baby food out of the cupboard and placed the jars in plain sight on the counter. She stood and thought. Then she took Brittany's favorite spoon and put it in front of the jars. She stared at the spoon, then at the garbage disposal, had a bad feeling, and dug out the two spoons Brittany sometimes accepted. She set them apart from the favorite, then she wondered if this spatial code was clear, and finally she wrote an explanatory note and taped it to the counter. Something still wasn't right. She stared at the fridge. She went over, moved the milk and bread and margarine to the front, and slid all the other clutter to the rear like a cop pushing back a crowd. She put her husband's favorite cereal on the counter, next to his Los Angeles Lakers bowl. Then she thought, shook her head, sighed, grabbed a spoon from the drawer and tossed it into his bowl. "Two points," she muttered. She wrote a note on using the microwave, then expanded this to four strips of paper, taped next to the relevant buttons. Same for the dishwasher. Next came two 8½-by-11 sheets walking him through the washer and dryer. She opened two suitcase-sized packages of disposable diapers and made eight stacks of six on Brittany's dresser. She wrote "Not for cooking!" on the bottle of baby oil. She taped the five-day weather forecast to the wall and set out clothes in clearly marked categories, without which he'd probably tie shoes on Brittany's hands. Next, she found the owner's guide to the stroller and left it open to "Getting to Know Your BabyMax F-90 Luxury Edition Stroller." In the bathtub, she made a line with a grease pencil, then wrote, "No water above here." She paused, then she added, "Avoid leaving B. unattended." She stared at this, knew it wouldn't overpower the pull of the Golf Channel on TV, erased it, and wrote instead, "Don't let our beautiful daughter drown!!!" She wrote her cell number on pieces of masking tape and stuck them on all the phones in the house. She highlighted a map of Encino, showing the routes to the emergency room, the pediatrician, the drugstore, the grocery store, and other destinations new to him. Then she drove to the airport.

Brittany stayed with a neighbor that afternoon. Her father picked her up after work. Dinner and breakfast went fine. This morning, driving her to her daycare, he had an unfamiliar, satisfied glow from doing his fatherly duty. He had her Raffi tape playing, her car seat crammed with toys. He felt a solidarity with the other parents on the freeway, practically waved at a stunning, auburn-haired mother in a new BMW wagon—and then traffic stopped.

That was an hour ago. The car has since been planted in Cheerios, flung in all directions like sown seed. The leather is still beaded in dozens of places from Brittany's successful opening of her water cup. Wet ink from her mother's note on car-seat safety is still running down and *staining the left leg of her eighty-dollar playsuit. The moment the engine went off, she began kicking and screaming. Her father turned up the music, switched to radio, tried to interest her in the sports news, quieted her for a minute and a half by playing with the electric windows, and finally had to release her from her car seat. He's phoned the insurance company where he works, told them he'll be late, and now drums his fingers louder and louder on the dash. He has calls to make, work to do. Without work, life is meaningless—a forkful of air instead of lasagna. And nothing, not a thousand-car pileup, not his own offspring driving him crazy with her rattle, is going to keep him from his work.*

Brittany starts wailing. She's got teeth coming in, but he mistakenly rubbed the gum-numbing medication on her lips this morning, thinking it was lip balm. He turns around, puts her back into her car seat, pries her sweaty fingers off the rattle, and sticks her teething ring in her mouth. "You do your work, and I'll do mine, OK? I want to see two more teeth before dinner! Got it?" His voice is still a novelty to her. She stops crying and listens. "Good."

He opens his briefcase, takes out the list of policyholders due for insurance checkups, and dials the first number on his cell phone.

"Mrs. Ramchandani? Did I pronounce that correctly?"

"Not really, but continue." She has an Indian accent.

"Real good." He produces a chuckle on demand. "Close enough for country music." He heard a tuning guitar player use this line at a bluegrass concert but suddenly wonders if it made any sense at all to his client. "Anyway, good morning to you! This is Bill Horbeck with Allstate Insurance. It's been a few years since we reviewed your coverages, and I'm—"

Brittany's teething ring hits him in the back of the head.

"—just calling to find out—"

His daughter bursts into a full-throated cry. He paws through his briefcase, finds a Power Bar, tears open the wrapper, and rams it in her mouth.

"—calling to find out if anything's changed with you and Mr. Ramchandani. Possibly—"

He hears a deep gurgling, whirls around, and sees he pushed the bar too far in and caused Brittany to gag and vomit. A second eruption follows, studded with Cheerios, flowing into a lake between her legs. He searches the glove compartment one-handed and finds only a single paper napkin.

"Maybe a change in assets. Maybe a need for more health insurance. Possibly a—perhaps you might have a new baby in the family." He forces another chuckle. The vomit has swallowed up the napkin. He sweeps his free

hand under the seat, pulls out the rag he checks the oil with, and sops up the mess as fast as he can, unaware of the black stains he's getting on her clothes.

"New baby? Are you crazy? My husband died last year!"

He flips the rag over and uses the dry side. "Is that right." He attempts to close his nose to the smell. Then her words register. He tries to place the Ramchandanis in his mind, but can't. He inherited them from an agent who retired. "I'm so sorry to hear that." He holds the reeking rag, unsure what to do with it, then uses his left elbow to lower his window and discreetly drops it outside on the ground. It lands with a conspicuous plop. The woman one car over stares at him. He raises the window.

"Did he——" He smells his hand, grimaces, looks in vain for water, then cradles the cell phone with his shoulder, lowers the window again, sticks his hand out, and pours the last of his cold coffee over it. "Did he have his life insurance with us? And if he did, could I ask how you'd rate our service?"

 An ambulance struggled to squeeze between the fast lane and the median. Del clambered into the passenger seat, switched on the radio, and searched for news. Stock prices, strings of golden oldies, DJ banter, call-ins, ads—the world of radio rolled on as before, a noisy party with the drapes closed, taking no notice of her predicament. It was an ever-flowing freeway all its own, crowded with sound, speed-loving—"Time for one more quick call," "Back with sports in thirty seconds." She was stuck, by contrast, in a spot where the unit of time was the hour.

She flicked the knob off in disgust and unfolded her crisp Arizona map. Roads fixed on paper, rivers stamped in blue, peaks marked permanently in place with an X: Maps were a realm outside of time, comforting in their permanence. She found Phoenix, then traveled north with her eyes, feeling herself gain in altitude, climbing into the green of the national forests. The shading on the map and the muscled bends in roads spoke clearly of mountains. There were campgrounds sprinkled about, and thousands of square miles of country where she could surely pitch her tent without paying a dime. She saw herself driving into a little one-store town to buy food from time to time. Scanning the map, Del wondered if it might turn out to be Happy Jack, or Perkinsville, or Pine. The four days spent camping in the Sierras with her foster family two summers before had been great, and she reminded herself how much she'd loved it. In the Datsun's trunk she had fishing gear, a hatchet, matches, a used copy of *The Boy Scout Handbook.* She would live off the land as much as she could. In winter, she'd move south to a warmer site.

She had a cell phone—prepaid, so no bill would come to Opal's—bought with the money saved by skipping car insurance. When she needed money for gas and supplies she could do telemarketing, phone sex, all kinds of jobs that just required a phone. She'd also copied an 800 number off a "Work At Home" ad on a telephone pole.

But what if the jam held her up so long that she couldn't make it to the mountains that night? She chewed on a fingernail. Blowing money on a motel was out. The phone had left her only $134. She'd left her credit card behind—transactions would give her away. To avoid looking like a runaway, she'd left her bank account open and $10 in it. She wished she had that extra money now. She studied the map. Then she spotted the green triangles. She could sleep at a rest stop. People did that all the time. Her door locks worked. She'd be safe. That is, as long as it wasn't in the desert and so hot that she had to leave her windows open. She considered. She'd try to park near a family.

"'No man is an island, entire of itself,'" her English teacher's voice recited in her head.

If there weren't any families, she'd look for another woman. Or anyone who looked safe.

"I really, *really* need to get going," Del informed the universe.

She returned to the map, then found herself staring at the personalized license plate in front of her. It read "Doopsie." Weird nickname, she thought. Then out loud she spoke her new name: "Elena Franco"— Elena from a Dostoevsky novel, a name she'd always thought beautiful, Franco from the singer Ani DiFranco. It was no less legitimate than Audelia Thigpen, given her by her first foster parents, who'd decided not to adopt her after all but had left her saddled with their distasteful, teasing-friendly surname. "Elena Franco." She said it in her head over and over. You could go by any name you wanted. Someday, when it was safe, she'd change it legally. Softly, she spoke the name aloud four times, to accustom her mouth to its contours. If a cop shined his light into her car at night, she'd have to have the right name on her tongue. She said it again. Then she looked up into the mirror, as if facing another person. "Headed east," she spoke up. "How 'bout you?" Then, "I always sleep at rest stops. Saves money, you know?"

She figured that if the jam lasted till noon, she'd probably need those lines. And that would depend on the accident. For the first time, she looked at the rows of cars before her and realized someone had probably died at the head of the line. If her car had been

41

faster, she might have been the one. "'Never send to know for whom the bell tolls,'" spoke her English teacher in her head. Del finished the line out loud: "'It tolls for thee.'"

I check out the accident. There's a huge semi sticking through the median, blocking three lanes northbound and one to the south. A crushed Camaro affixed to the truck's cab. Various cars and smaller trucks dented or totaled, scattered about. One car's on its hood, like a bug on its back. It's a tornado scene. Injured drivers, paramedics, police, firemen, tow trucks, helicopters. I hear someone say that the woman in the Camaro is dead. In my head, I hear the words, "No man is an island."

No man is an island? Tell that to the car makers. You've got your Chevy Corsica. Your Catalina. Your Capri. "Yeah, we decided on the Ford Madagascar. It had more legroom than the Maui." The whole lure of cars is the idea that they're islands. Completely self-contained realms. You look in the windows of the new cars at a dealer and you say, "Oooh, I want to live there." They're houses in miniature. You've got your easy chair next to your sound system, a phone, bathroom mirror, furnace and A/C, political signs out on the lawn, lighting, carpeting, attic storage in the trunk, all guarded by a security system. And each one customized to the owner's tastes. Looking down at the cars, it hits me that I might as well be looking up—at the Milky Way, at endless separate worlds.

One car in particular catches my eye, a planet like no other. It's old. From the forties or fifties. And it's big, built to a scale I'm not used to, a dinosaur among terriers. No sharp corners, all its ends rounded off, like a muffin rising. The car's body has a low hem to it—so low the rear fenders cover half the wheels. There's an elegance about it, the spaciousness of a limo. You'd expect a mob boss in a tux to step out the rear door. It's black and shiny. The chrome grill is immaculate. It looks like it hasn't been driven since a cup of coffee cost a dime.

I fly low to look closer. I'm not the only one. A man from a Volvo, two cars over, is checking it out in ecstasy, running his eyes and hands over it as if over his newborn child. He's the third visitor that hour. In the car's front seat, the driver is still clutching the wheel and cursing his luck. He feels another rivulet of sweat roll down his back. He stole the car that morning.

"A Hudson Hornet!" the Volvo owner exclaims. "What is it—a '51?"

The driver's face is stiff as wood. He's eighteen, an illegal from northern Mexico. He has the windows up. He stares blankly ahead, pretending not to notice the man, not to understand English, not to be in the car. He checks the mirror for the millionth time for cops. He closes his eyes and sends the Virgin of Guadalupe a prayer she rarely gets—to whisk him back to the Sonoran desert.

"High-compression six-cylinder—right?" The Volvo owner's puffy face looms into view, pressed up to the driver's window as if he's a fish in an aquarium. "Right?"

The driver knows nothing about the car but nods, hoping the man will leave. He doesn't.

"My father used to race these when he was a kid!"

The driver has a sudden vision of himself when he was young, leaning against his mother. She's at the stove, stirring sopa de ajo, *garlic soup, steam rising and making her cheeks glisten. He wishes he'd never left her side.*

"Perimeter frame, right?"

He can't believe he's stuck in the jam two exits before his destination. But he is. He was born without luck, on the same day his father was crushed to death by his own truck while he worked on the brakes. Superstitious relatives had blamed the newborn boy. His uncles avoided him. Things broke around him. Knobs came off in his hand. Weather turned bad when he looked at the sky. He was angry with his role, didn't know what he'd done to deserve it. His uncles encouraged him to cross the border when he was fifteen. They blamed him for the past three years of drought. Hoped the kid would take it with him up north.

The Volvo owner is still there. "The floor on the same level with the chassis? Right?"

The driver gives a feeble nod. Loud, pushy, car-mad gringos. He hears another helicopter, glances up, and knows his car sticks out like an eggplant among oranges. Helicopters have been going over all day. He's sure he's been spotted. He closes his eyes again, sees himself being knifed in a prison yard, and decides to keep them open instead.

"What did they call it? The Step-Down design?"

The driver gives no response. He wishes he were picking strawberries like his cousin, imagines himself out in the open air, birds singing, beautiful Augustina Reynosa from tenth grade beside him. Her family picked. Why hadn't he gone with them? Instead, he was sleeping under the kitchen table in a one-bedroom apartment with nine other people, buffing supermarket floors all night, breathing fumes from the chemicals, getting less than minimum wage from the labor contractor, stumbling into school in a daze. One of the other men in the apartment had told him about the car. He'd been promised $100 once he delivered it. He'd never stolen anything in his life. He asks his mother to forgive him. He begs the Virgin to lift him up and set him down in the strawberry fields.

"You don't mind if I—" The Volvo owner doesn't bother to finish his sentence but just opens the left rear door and climbs in.

"It's true! You step down when you go inside!"

The driver turns around, wants to scream at the man to leave, but can't afford to draw any further attention to himself. The man bounces on the seat, like a balding, three-piece-suited toddler.

"More comfortable than my brand-new Volvo! It's amazing!"

Three cars back, a beefy refrigerator repairman can't contain his curiosity any longer. He extracts himself from his minuscule Mitsubishi pickup, ambles forward, puts his red face to the passenger window, and jerks his head in greeting to the driver while he brazenly ogles the interior.

"Some car," he says. His voice is muffled by the glass. The driver recognizes this as a preview of his prison visits with outsiders.

"You oughta try out the seats!" says the Volvo driver.

The repairman opens the right rear door. The driver feels the car sink down. With his luck, a rear tire will blow.

"It's like a goddamn living room in here," says the repairman. He spreads his arms over the top of the burgundy velour seats and inhales with gusto. "Not like that iron lung I'm driving."

How did these people get into his car? the driver asks himself. He's desperate to get rid of them but has no idea how. He feels like maggots are crawling under his clothes. He pleads with the Virgin to vaporize the men.

"How long you had it?" the repairman asks him.

The driver grinds his teeth. He knows that not answering would instantly raise their suspicion. The first time he was asked, he answered "Two weeks," then thought this sounded too short. The next time, he made it two years, then four, and now avoids the question completely by answering, "Actually, it's my dad's." He's never used the word "dad" before. He learned English in high school in East L.A. but tries now to sound as suburban as possible. "He likes old cars."

"Just like my dad!" says the Volvo owner. He opens and closes the ashtray in the door. "You just taking it out to keep the oil moving? Give the tranny a little work?"

The driver feels like he's being strip-searched. He works at seeming calm. "Yeah. The oil." He files this explanation in his memory.

A police car, siren blaring, shoots up the empty southbound lanes. The driver's blood pressure breaks his old record. He touches the shirt pocket that holds his fake driver's license, the one that came with the name he's never liked: Fernando Guyaba Guzman. He's had it three years and still isn't used to the name. He practices it quickly now in his head.

"I swear, you could sit four back here," says the repairman.

The Volvo owner is impressed with the gadgetless serenity. "It's so calm inside, you know?" He feels a surge of desire to divest his car of its cell phone, Fuzzbuster, fax, CD player, and its chatty onboard computer. He turns to the repairman. "So where were you headed? To work?"

The driver feels ready to explode. Was it a car he was driving or a social club? His teeth grind like glaciers. Just two more exits to the man with the truck, who was supposed to haul the car out of state. He should have been there an hour ago. He'd have called except that the cell phone they'd loaned him had fallen out of his shirt pocket and smashed to pieces during the heist. A fresh trickle of sweat picks its way down his rib cage. To the right, a woman, tired of sitting, gets out of her Saab and wanders over.

"What is this thing anyway?"

The driver rolls his eyes. He has no strength left for dealing with people but doesn't have a choice. He rolls down his window a few inches. "My dad—" His voice is too dry. He swallows. "My dad calls it the Tank." He congratulates himself on avoiding the car's make, in case she's got a police scanner. He keeps his voice low. "'Cause it's big." He pauses, then tries to lose her down a conversational alley. "He drove a tank. In one of the wars."

"It's a '51 Hudson Hornet!" crows the Volvo driver for the world to hear. "And it's a beauty. Come on in!"

Two lanes over, a gray-goateed man in a black suit got out of his Mercedes. He didn't go anywhere but just lit a cigarette and leaned against his fender, elegant as a statue.

What is it, a nonsmoking car? thought Del. She watched him bring the cigarette to his lips. "Smoking is such an *art*," she said out loud. It was a branch of dance. A tango for one. Then a door shut behind her. She looked in the mirror and saw two men exit their windowless van. A few minutes later, the SUV in front of her rolled down its windows.

"Batteries," Del said aloud. They couldn't run their air conditioning forever. She turned and looked behind her. The freeway was hatching out. People were emerging, stretching, peering ahead and behind, fanning themselves.

Del returned to the rear seat, grabbed a soda from her ice chest, and watched the scene out the back window. A woman walked a golden retriever. Two gardeners washed their truck windows with water and newspaper. The empty lanes began wriggling with life. Some people struck up conversations with others; most loitered alone by their cars, especially, Del noticed, if the car was expensive.

"Snobs," she sneered. They had to let the world know what they were driving, had to maintain the hierarchy here, among strangers, lest they lose their identities. Make and model were like genus and species, with subspecies differentiated by year, horsepower, leather, accessories. Drivers rested crossed arms on their roofs, reclined against doors, maintained the connection. Looking at the Mercedes driver to her left, Del could hardly tell where his black suit stopped and the car's black body began.

"If you've got it," she imitated Zero Mostel from *The Producers*, "flaunt it."

Back and to the right, a woman in a business suit climbed out of an Audi, opened a water bottle, and took a long drink. It was then that Del noticed how few women had left their cars. Del spotted two men watching the water drinker. She might have been on stage. Are they gonna yell "Encore," Del wondered, when she finishes? She was impressed by the woman. Somehow, men seemed to own public space and felt no qualms about inhabiting it; women needed an invitation or a companion. "What's that about?" Del asked herself out loud. She counted four different women in SUVs, all of whom preferred to remain in their castles.

"Wimps," she mocked them. Not that she had plans for leaving her own car. What would she do? Who would she talk to? The thought took her back to that dreaded first morning each time she entered a new school, furtively scanning the different groups, wondering if she should stand with the blacks or whites or Hispanics or off by herself, hating the feeling of being watched, hating always being new and alone. Up through sixth grade, she'd striven for invisibility at school. Then she'd discovered the benefits of a boyfriend. Someone to stand next to. Someone to eat with, call up, write seven-page notes to, a phone number to worship, a name to inscribe ornately on desks. Suddenly, you were a relative in the school family: Brandon's girlfriend, Rico's girlfriend. Finding a boy became her first order of school business, in front of sharpening her pencils. It wasn't hard. Her adult body had arrived early. All you had to do was let them touch your breasts. Her own demands were more extensive: to know everything about them, to keep in constant contact, to live inside them like a lodger, to believe in their undying loyalty—the sort in short supply in seventh grade, especially among boys feeling smothered. Her relationships had all been brittle. She was always the one dumped, a devastation that could only be numbed by something as strong as another crush. She was drawn toward boys from stand-ard families, was continually amazed at their taken-for-granted identities, at how long they'd known their best friends and lived at their addresses. The same cycle continued into high school, until she'd finally become disheartened with it all, confronting the last boy who'd told her to stop calling, cursing him out at the top of her voice in the cafeteria a few months before. Her best friend of late had been a gay guy a year ahead, another outsider. And Mr. Carbon in chemistry.

A man with a loosened tie and a ponytail sauntered up to the Mercedes driver and began talking. Del watched the conversational kindling ignite into sudden laughter, and tried seeing the scene around her as Mr. Carbon would: bonds forming and dissolving, inert personalities remaining in their cars, the heat and compression from crowding encouraging reactions. Among teachers, Del was renowned for the size of both her intellect and her attitude. Math and science, however, weren't her thing. She'd expected to hate chemistry and Mr. Carbon but instead found he was giving her x-ray glasses, showing her the hidden structure of the world. In turn, she suspected that he could see her structure, her own valence, ravenous for electrons, that he could see into her unquenchable anger just as he knew what fueled the sun's fires. They'd talked several times after class. She'd never gotten anything out of her therapists, hated their attempts to get to know her, and had finally refused to go. Visiting Mr. Carbon was voluntary. With his plaid bow ties and crooked smile and chalky hands, he seemed an unlikely confidant. Yet he seemed as genuinely curious about his students' lives as about proteins and peptides. She'd imitated Opal for him and had enjoyed her ability to make him laugh. She was surprised by how much she told him and embarrassed that he'd witnessed her cafeteria outburst. In his room after school that day, he took up his wooden pointer and stood before the periodic table.

"There he is. See him?"

She didn't know what he was talking about.

"Justin Doyle, your former knight in shining armor. A smart kid. But the kind who likes to have more than one girl at a time, from what I've seen. I'd put him here"—he tapped the table—"among the halogens. Quite a popular category of male, actually. Always available and extremely reactive. Maybe that's why so many females go shopping there."

She chewed on what he'd said. He turned back toward the table. "But I have a prediction, Del." He touched the middle of the table with his pointer. "Someday you'll do your shopping somewhere over here. Where the more stable males reside. You won't be drawn to the halogens—because you yourself will have changed your address on the table. Changed your number of valence electrons." He looked at her. "Prediction, not advice."

He smiled, then softened his voice. "And someday, when life doesn't give you what you want, you won't have quite such a violent reaction." He thought back to her tirade. "Intense heat. Flames. That sort of thing."

Del lowered her eyes, embarrassed at herself.

"But I have another prediction for you. That someday all that raging energy of yours will turn turbines and light cities." He paused. "I don't know when and I don't know how. But something tells me that it's so."

She looked and listened with the sum of her senses, as if hearing her destiny read aloud.

I had a chemistry teacher who used to say, "Change is the essence of the universe." I find myself thinking about him, because flying through the air's changed my brain. I'm not the same person. It's incredibly calming. It's like getting a transfusion with wine. "We're all out of O-negative, Doctor." "Well then, give her three liters of Beaujolais." I'm at peace. I've forgotten all about maybe missing my flight. It's like someone dragged an eraser over my memory. I'm not obsessing about my daughter's sixth birthday party back in Boulder in three days. Not a thought about Lola down the block, who's taking care of her. Or Greg, next door, who's feeding and walking our dogs. Everybody needs a neighborhood like mine—especially every single

parent who's trying to make it in the arts. I'm not thinking about my agent, who says he read my last play three times but still calls me Elaine instead of Elena. I've forgotten about work, heating bills, rent. I'm soaring, swooping, parting the air with my face. Reveling in my x-ray vision and hearing. Losing myself entirely in other people's lives.

Southbound. Fast lane. A green Acura. An Amnesty International decal on one end of the bumper. On the other end, "Skateboarding Is Not a Crime." It's one of the few cars containing more than one human, a rare double-yolker. Mother and fifteen-year-old son. People used to have kids because they needed help on the farm. In L.A., you have kids so you can use the carpool lane.

I hear the mother clearing her throat, very softly. Then again, just a bit louder. A signal for the imminent arrival of words, like a train being announced at the station. The mother chooses her voice settings. She flicks the switches for Cheery, Nonjudgmental, and Nonchalant. She inhales and licks her lips. Then she starts. "I suppose we'll just have to make the best of it."

She looks up into the mirror. Her son, being driven to his private school in Westwood, has started sitting in the back lately. His eyes are on the game he's playing on his cell phone, in which a convertible tries to evade the falling excrement from a flock of seagulls.

"Then again, in my own life, quite often really, I've found that what appears on the surface to be bad news—"

He turns up the CD he's listening to through head-phones, blocking out most of her words.

"—the time we got the flat tire on the way to the Grand Canyon—"

He jerks the convertible to the left too late and gets bombed. The phone emits an electronic splat.

"—normal for adolescents to pull away. I remember when I—"

He switches CD tracks and bumps the volume up two more notches.

"—both your father and I—"

He gets bombed again, fires an accusing glance at his mother, then checks his score: 9 hits, 33 seconds remaining.

"—communication is so—"

Two more hits. He rolls his eyes.

"—make use of the chance to just talk for a change."

Another hit. He absolutely can't play while she's yapping. He jabs at a button and pauses the game. "Talk about what?"

She shrugs off his tone and smiles up at the mirror. "Anything. Whatever you want to talk about. If you wouldn't mind taking off your headphones for just—"

"I can hear fine with them on."

"But Brice—"

"I can hear you! Trust me! That's why I've got bird crap all over me!"

She whirls around and checks his green sweater and navy pants, the school uniform. "You've got what?"

"Never mind! Let's get this over with!"

"Well, it would be common courtesy if you'd take off your headphones for just a few—"

"We just went over that! Don't you listen?"

She turns back toward the front. "All I'm saying—"

Brice rips them off his head and throws them on his lap. "There! OK! Are you happy now?"

She sighs. She props up her smile. "Anyway, I just thought that we could make use—"

"You already said that."

She gets tired of aiming her eyes up at the mirror. She lowers them and faces the round, side-by-side gauges for fuel and temperature. "So what would you like to talk about?"

"Nothing. There. Are we done now?"

Miniature voices are shrieking from the headphones. "Would you mind turning off the heavy metal for a minute?"

"It's techno, not heavy metal!" He laughs uproariously. She turns around in her seat, sees the greenish tinge to his teeth, considers beginning with a discussion of brushing, but restrains herself. She faces the front. His laughter dies down after two and a half minutes.

"Heavy metal!"

"Pardon me." She pauses. "Now, if you'd kindly turn it off—"

"I can hear you just fine! I'm right here! Are you kidding?"

"Brice, please."

"I can't believe you!"

"Just out of politeness." She turns and faces him. *"So I know I have your full attention."*

The song ends. Silence descends. His mother closes her eyes in gratitude. *"Thank you."*

The next song starts. She snaps. *"Turn that off."*

He mutters, then turns it down to half its volume.

"I said off."

"It is off."

"It's not off. I can hear it!"

He turns it lower. *"Can you hear that?"*

"Yes," she lies.

He turns the volume to number one. *"How 'bout now?"*

Her left arm shoots forward. She snatches the CD player and its tentacles off his lap and slams it all down on the passenger seat. She closes her eyes, then spends half a minute trying to slow her breathing. She emerges from this session stone-faced. Her voice is unnaturally soft.

"I thought . . . we might . . . have a simple—"

His cell phone rings. He answers instantaneously. *"Hey . . .Yeah. Us, too . . . No kidding . . . Don't ask . . . Chillin' with my mom, who's like completely weirded out by being stuck and like wants to psychoanalyze me. Hold on, I've got another call . . ."*

Del's eye fell on the magazines she'd bought at a thrift store—a *Seventeen,* a *National Geographic,* two issues of *Mother Earth News.* She picked up one of the latter and scanned the table of contents: "Growing Rosemary for Fun and Profit," "Build Your Own Fretless Banjo," "Septic System Troubleshooting—Part 2." She thought of her twelve-pack of toilet paper. That and a folding shovel would be her septic system. Maybe she wasn't in *Mother Earth*'s league. She was a hunter-gatherer, not a farmer. Her car and tent would be her home, a home she moved from place to place, like the Plains Indians with their teepees. Del dropped the magazine. Her eye flitted about the car. If this was her home, it was time to make it her own.

She yanked off the depressing air freshener. Died fighting L.A.'s smog single-handed, she thought. She stuffed it in a bag she designated for trash. Then she opened up her pocket knife and worked her way around the inside of the windows, scraping off oil-change reminders, parking stickers, laughable security-system warnings, decals with mysterious acronyms. There were three on the outside of the windshield. She dispatched them, got back inside, and was amazed at the difference it made, as if she'd just washed a room's filthy windows. Del looked lovingly at her knife, one of the few things bought new, carefully cleaned the gummy blade, and rolled the windows back down to let in the breeze. She felt better.

Two men walked past her, talking politics, one with a pungent New York accent. She stared at the parka on the back seat, wondered how that would look to others, then plunged into giving the car a makeover, from Runaway's Hideout to Vacationmobile. Winter clothes, serious groceries—the six jars of peanut butter, twenty-four bottles of water, the nearly complete set of Campbell's soups—went into the trunk and out of sight. She moved her ice chest back to keep it colder, making room in the trunk by bringing forward her tarp and tent and camp stove. These she fitted nicely into place on the floor. On the back seat she spread a blanket and smoothed out the wrinkles. She put a pillow in one corner and Lassie in the other, then displayed in the rear window the books she'd brought along: the Molière plays, the Tupac biography, some science fiction, *Les Misérables,* a couple of graphic novels for fun. If anyone asked, she'd say she was in college, doing some camping in the Southwest.

She couldn't stop herself. She went through the covered holdall between the front seats, the glove compartment, the map slots in the doors, the grimy dungeon under the seats—cleaning, tossing, declaring ownership. She'd never felt any of her rooms were hers, had never decided what went where, had never known how long she'd be staying. This was hers. She used paper napkins and her water bottle to clean the dusty dash, then the steering wheel, then everything in sight. She fed her change into the hidden coin holder, proud of her little stack of quarters. The car was from the pre-cupholder era, but someone had added a clip-on to the console. She folded a napkin to catch drips, placed it inside, and then her bottle. She put her knife in the glove compartment, then decided she preferred it at her side, in the holder between the seats. She could make up whatever rules she wanted.

Del rested. Then she turned on the ignition, climbed out, and began checking her lights. Getting pulled over would be a disaster. To halt suspicion that she'd run away, she'd had to leave her wallet behind. A month before, she'd gotten a duplicate driver's license. What she didn't have was car registration, which would have required a guardian's signature—impossible, since the car was a secret. Likewise, no proof of insurance.

She tried her turn signals, then moved her stove to the front and leaned it against the brake pedal while she checked the rear lights. Everything seemed to work, though it was hard to be sure in the bright sun. If bulbs were cheap, she'd buy some spares at a gas station. Not being eighteen, she could still be returned to Opal if the police found her. She wasn't about to let that happen because of a burned-out license-plate light.

She lay down in the back and surveyed the car with pleasure, then opened the *National Geographic.* She wasn't sure why she'd bought it—maybe because of the cover photo of the Sahara. She flipped forward to the cover story. After a morning squeezed among thousands of cars and a lifetime spent among L.A.'s millions, she was drawn to the Sahara's endless spaces, inhabited only by the wind. She reached for her knife, pried out its tiny scissors, carefully cut out a photo, snipped a piece of adhesive tape from her first-aid kit, and taped the picture to the back of the passenger seat. She leaned back, gazed at it, and grinned. She no longer felt so confined. She found a similar wide-angle scene for the driver's seat and began to cut.

"Decorator crab," she said out loud. She'd seen it in her biology book the year before, a crab that covers itself with plants, other creatures, anything it can find. It was something she'd been doing for years. How good it had felt to declare herself a fan of *The Simpsons,* to carry her Lisa Simpson binder to school, to act out scenes from the show at recess. In the same way, she'd become a regular reader of *Calvin and Hobbes,* a fan of a panoply of music groups, a devoted viewer of *The Real World,* firmly attaching song lyrics and scenes to herself with her powerful memory. At one school, she'd been nicknamed "Jukebox" for her feats of memorization. She could sing ten-minute, word-crammed rap songs without missing a syllable, knew the words to gospel songs she hadn't heard in years, could still recite Bill Cosby routines from the comedy albums at her fifth house—all serving to cover her bare walls. She'd winked at the decorator crab, wondering if any of the other students even noticed it. It was all she remembered of biology.

She taped the second photo in place, a sunset-reddened landscape, the sky empty of clouds, planes, traffic helicopters. She began to fall into the scene, then was yanked out by her neighbor on the right talking on his cell phone.

"That's what they said. On the radio."

Del sat up, openly eavesdropping.

"Three or four more hours! *Minimum!* Probably longer for eastbound."

Del realized she was in the eastbound lanes. She fell back down in her seat as if shot. She felt she'd done enough yelling already, almost kicked the door but didn't want to hurt the car. In the jukebox of her brain, someone pushed the button for "Don't Worry, Be Happy." She heard Bobby McFerrin's alluring accent but refused to sing along with the song.

"Shut up!" she finally yelled at it.

The man next to her quickly lowered his voice, then rolled up his window.

She climbed forward and searched her radio for news, to drown out the song and in hopes of a different verdict. She found a report on the crash: two trucks and eleven cars, a spill of liquid pesticides from one of the trucks, one dead and several major injuries, no crane as yet for moving the trucks. Accident investigators, said the announcer, often needed hours to measure and photograph and interview. This, Del realized, explained why people felt free to stroll. They could run a freaking marathon and still be back at their cars early. She snapped off the radio and lay down in the back.

She gazed at the copy of *Seventeen* for five minutes, then finally picked it up. The issue was three years old, packed with passé fashions that elicited rolled eyes, disbelieving squints, and her full vocabulary of snorts. "If you could see yourself," she mocked a model out loud. How superior they acted, how proud of their hem lengths and hairstyles now known to have been pathetic. "Don't be late," she sneered at two school-bound beauties, their backpacks probably filled with newspaper instead of fifty pounds of textbooks. "Tell 'em I won't be back in the fall." She turned pages with a noisy snap, as if slapping model after model. Most were blond, all with perfect features.

She positioned her face in the rearview mirror. Her own mix-and-match collection made her think of one of Picasso's cubist paintings: a cheekbone sticking out here, a too-wide nose there, ears too big, jaw too long, a chin as square as a man's. The multiethnic look was hot—but only if you were beautiful, which she wasn't. She dropped the magazine on the floor.

When she sat up, two hours later, she scented coconut oil in the air.

Del glanced about. The same cars were in place around her, but their drivers had vanished. The man in the Lexus and the cell phone talker were both gone. The freeway resembled a county fair, full of people milling around. She'd fallen asleep, making up for scarcely sleeping at all the night before. Now she was hot, thirsty, and had to pee. She wondered what everyone else was doing for a bathroom. It was time to find out.

She checked herself in the mirror. Chances of being seen by someone she knew, much less being recognized without her long hair, were infinitesimal. She adjusted her hat, grabbed her water bottle, and climbed out of the car.

A dragon-breathed breeze met her, instantly parching her skin. Reptilian scales, she thought, would have been a good fashion choice today. She drank from her bottle, trying to look around without being seen, as if she'd just slipped into a school dance. The garbage men had peeled down to their undershirts and were chatting up a woman passing by. Hip-hop was playing in the distance. Down the lane, she saw a man working on his car, two kids playing hop-scotch, a badminton birdie in the air. Her bladder felt heavy as an overdue baby. She raised her windows and locked the car. A shirtless teenager reading a magazine while he walked came toward her.

"How ya doin'?" he said.

"Great!" She felt flustered. "It's great."

He passed her. Del closed her eyes. What was great about being stuck here for hours? He must have thought she was deranged. Then she saw the earphone wires leading to his ears. Maybe he hadn't even heard her. She set off in the opposite direction.

Bummer, she coached herself. And it's broiling, of course. Going camping. If we ever get out of here. Elena. Hi. Elena Franco.

 For some, the jam's a chance to change their identities. They're cut off from everyone they know. Their biographies have been miraculously deleted. It's an opportunity to start over, to imagine new lives, to act like the people

they'd always wished they were. For others, the leisure for self-reflection is a curse. It's an unexpected appointment with themselves. Hour after hour of staring into a mirror— and not liking what they see.

Soaring through the air, I hear a woman's voice. Loud as a car alarm, wailing through tears. "I CAN'T BELIEVE THIS! . . ." I peer through the roof of her Toyota Corolla. She's strangling the steering wheel. Kicking at the floor. Seems to have some issues around anger. Either that or she's giving birth. A gigantic groan. I want to tell her to push. Then a Hitchcock scream. And out it comes.

"I . . . HATE . . . MY . . . LIFE!"

Then the afterbirth, mumbled rapid-fire under her breath with eyes closed, like a memorized prayer.

"I'll be five hours late to my new temp assignment, another first-day late arrival, the third one this month, none of them my fault, but who cares, I'll lose the job, my agency will fire me and put in my file, "Unreliability a problem," I don't last long enough to be called a temp, I'm an ephemeral, 'So what do you do?' 'I'm a phem.'

"I have to work so I can afford the payments, gas, insurance, and repairs on this car, which I bought so I can get to work. Why don't cars go out and get their own god- damn jobs?

"On the day when I make the last car payment the car will die, no surprise, it's got nothing left to live for, it's

paid itself off, it's a mother salmon who's laid her eggs, floating in a daze, it's all part of nature, like the water cycle, old cars evaporating, new cars raining down from Japan.

"Both my sisters are married and have children, my brother is married and has children, I'm 38, I have a guinea pig, I'm a spinster, in California you can't legally call yourself an elder or wise woman until you're fifty-nine and a half.

"'Find a nice man,' my mother suggests helpfully, but the available men are available for a reason: lemons, police auction items, pre-pre-pre-owned, undisclosed accidents, factory recalls, and yet they pick you, not the other way around, and what they want ideally is a woman who'll drive them to the mechanic to pick up their car, which is always much nicer than yours and takes premium gas, therefore they want a woman with a car, therefore a woman with a job, which I just lost!"

She opens her eyes and glares at the huge Apple Computer billboard to her right with its two-word slogan, "Think Different." She's a word person, a glasses-wearing former editor, copyeditor, proofreader, a writer in margins of library books, a guerrilla warrior on the front between good grammar and chaos, a woman who dumped her last suitor, two years before, for giving her a Valentine candy that read "Your mine." Y-O-U-R, no apostrophe, no e. She underlines run-on sentences and faulty agreements in the L.A. Times *and sends them back to the writers but can't keep up. Flogging them for their sins would be a full-time job. She's already written to Apple, on the letterhead of her one-woman watchdog group, the Society for the Prevention of Cruelty to English, but she's never received a reply. She narrows her eyes and sends a death ray at the billboard.*

"Try writing different*!" she yells at it.*

She turns on the radio, looks for an update on the jam, speeds past the classical music on KUSC. Her father teaches violin at USC, her mother teaches cello, her siblings all play instruments. She herself has no musical talent, the one Bach kid who went into farming. Her parents are demanding and detail oriented. Both tried to teach her their instruments, both threw up their hands within weeks. Both had dreamed of a family string sextet. Her homeliness was a further disappointment to her mother— not to mention her temper, sleeping habits, diet, choice of reading, choice of friends, choice of clothes, choice of radio stations. This tide of maternal advice has still not gone out. There's an assumption of rightness in her mother's voice that she finds maddening. Arguing with her is like arguing with a metronome.

She finds a radio report on the jam. The words are identical to the last report she heard. She realizes the newscaster isn't live, as she'd thought, and feels duped and stupid the way you do when you take a store man-

nequin for a real person and start to ask it where the bathrooms are. She punches off the radio, digs into a Hostess Twinkie, and prays to the health and beauty gods for forgiveness. She's an atheist but believes fervently in obesity and heart disease. She's five foot five, twenty pounds overweight but has no interest in exercise. Why display her disgusting body to the world? Jogging is for people who don't need to. She checks out her long, lifeless hair in the mirror while she eats. Her last home dyeing job left streaks of gray showing through the brown. Her head looks like a finger painting. Clairol hasn't responded to her letter, marked EXTREMELY URGENT. She pinches her cheek. Her skin's pale and doughy, no longer fastened tightly to her bones. Lines at the corners of her mouth are deepening into canyons. She thinks, My jaw looks like a ventriloquist's dummy's. She recalls an ad for a spray that gives old cars that new-car smell. She fantasizes spraying her entire body with it. She gulps down the Twinkie, flicks the mirror up to keep from seeing herself, and aims her eyes down at the new issue of Self.

She flips through it randomly, in ten-page chunks, too agitated to read. She turns to a column on retirement plans. Then she's in an article on underwear called "Thong of Solomon." She touches down on a perfume ad. Then she opens to a page of solid text, with two sentences blown up large: "Start where you are. If you're stuck, embrace stuckness." She stares at the words, snorts, thinks of the jam, rereads the words, flips back a page. The piece is about a Buddhist retreat on Puget Sound. The article's titled "Contemplate This" and deals with accepting our- selves as we are, with loving-kindness, then extending this compassion to the world at large. She reads it all and puts down the magazine. She flips the mirror back down, takes a strand of gray hair in her hand, and speaks the words, "I am what I am." She thinks to herself, I have gray hair. I weigh 157 pounds. She uses a neutral voice, giving these statements the sound of simple facts. My face has lines. My calves are thicker than I'd like. I don't play an instrument. Then she adds in her defense, I prefer to read in my spare time. I don't have a career. I don't have a hus- band. Then she adds, At the present time. She listens to how different this description sounds stripped of accusation. "I don't have a career," she says out loud. She regards the statement both ways, like an optical illusion: condemning, then accepting. "I don't have a husband at the present time." The words echo in her ears, spreading in concentric rings. "I am what I am." She feels as if her toes are touching land after years of frantic dog-paddling offshore. It's never occurred to her that she might be acceptable as she is. Her parents never encouraged such a view. They made her feel a constant failure. Then the thought hits her: They are what they are. She holds on to the steering wheel as if it's a life preserver. They are what they are. She knows it's true. As true as her gray hair and flabby thighs. They couldn't help being the way they were any more than they could help being musicians. They weren't virtuosos at child rearing. They were tone-deaf amateurs. They are what they are. The phrase circles her brain like a leaf in an eddy. Then she wonders, But why did I have to get them for parents? She takes in the endless rows of cars before her. As if in a trance, she says in reply, "The world is what it is." And she closes her eyes.

When she opens them, ten minutes later, she looks up at the billboard, at the words "Think Different." And she says nothing at all.

The lanes teemed like an Arab bazaar. Del entered and felt herself disappear into the labyrinth. She nodded at some of those strolling the other way, said "Hi" back to a few of the ones leaning against their cars, passed unnoticed through a hundred conversations. "A tumor, I'm not kidding, the size of . . ." "Rebuilt engine, new shocks, new transmission . . . " "But with a whole-life policy, you're not just getting insurance . . ." She moved over to the shoulder, where there was more room to walk, and smiled secretly. She was surrounded by strangers. No one here knew her from before. She was taken at face value. Those who nodded at her were nodding at Elena. She'd done the impossible—escaped her shadow on the sidewalk. The hidden smile leaked onto her lips.

"Hey, sunshine." A toad-faced man leered at her from the passenger seat of his carpet-cleaning van. He held out a business card. "Special rate, just for you."

She replaced her smile with a smirk and ignored him, leaving his hand hanging in midair. She took pleasure in this. Her new self, unlike her old, was a sovereign state. She could choose where to live and how, down to the details. Finally, she possessed the power to reject what she didn't like. She gloried in the feeling. She cut through the crowd with this broadsword, felt she was taking a farewell tour of Los Angeles, walking incognito among her tormentors, privately calling out, "Off with their heads!" How absurd they all were: the man using his cell phone, laptop, and PDA simultaneously. The blond sunbathing on the bed of the pickup in her bra and bikini underwear, willing to get skin cancer in exchange for a tan. The trio of bored thirty-somethings singing the *Gilligan's Island* song. The Jaguar owner painstakingly cleaning his hood ornament with a toothbrush and rag. The crowd pressed to the windows of a minivan so as to watch—along with the toddlers inside—a Winnie-the-Pooh cartoon on a drop-down screen. She thought to herself, They should remake *Ship of Fools* and call it *Freeway of Idiots*.

She passed a woman holding a toy poodle wearing its own little sun hat embroidered "Poodelicious." These were my neighbors, Del thought, even weirder than the crew on *Mr. Rogers' Neighborhood.* These were my teachers, social workers, parents. No wonder I've got an attitude. She thought of her foster mother who covered the house with instructions typed on index cards: "Turn Off Light Switch After Using." "Close Refrigerator Door After Opening." The father who chained her outside with the dog as a punishment for wetting the bed. The couple clearly in it for the money, with four foster kids, the kindergartner assigned to watch the baby, the seven-year-old watching the kindergartner, Del watching the seven-year-old, while the parents went out to movies. Opal teaching her to drive, instructing her to slow down before freeway overpasses to check for bowling-ball droppers. They were crazy. They weren't her parents any more than Pasadena, Alhambra, El Monte, Azusa, Glendale, Gardena, or Venice had been her home.

A walker in front of her had lit up a cigar, proudly announcing his pastime to hundreds of unimpressed breathers downwind. Del wrinkled her nose, couldn't believe it, then could. It's like dumping paint in a river, she thought. Which was probably the jerk's day job. Los Angeles—city of assholes, not angels. She crossed all five lanes to escape the stench, then climbed over the low cement median, crossed the empty westbound lanes, and took a seat on the guardrail. Staring out at the apartment houses without end, Del said a sour good-bye to it all. She closed her eyes. Then she wondered if her mother might be somewhere in the scene.

She found herself scanning windows, searching for a woman looking back at her. It was an old habit. It had always been a comfort to imagine her mother watching her. Her mixed background had allowed almost any woman to be a candidate. *Are You My Mother?* had been her favorite book for years. Since puberty, she'd imagined her mother resembling herself. It was the sole fact known about her, that she looked something like Del. She made contact with her each time she undressed, every time she looked into a mirror. She believed their periods were synchronized. Her father, by contrast, seemed too unknowable even for speculation. From the physique she shared with her mother, Del extrapolated a shared mind. She felt sure her mother had been drawn to the ocean and was as much a book lover as she was, often sensing while she was reading that her mother's eyes had previously traveled over each line. She ascribed noble motives to her mother in abandoning her and saved her anger for her foster stand-ins. Plots borrowed from soap operas and novels melted together in her mind. Her mother was the mistress of a powerful politician who couldn't afford a scandal. Her mother was a refugee from the fighting in Central America. Her mother's parents had demanded she get an abortion, but she'd refused to sacrifice Del. Del was heir to a Beverly Hills estate, half-sister to a movie star, a Dickensian waif unaware of her highborn relations. Only lately had she dared imagine darker scenarios: a drug-using runaway, a middle-school-aged mother, a West Side nanny raped by her employer. Even here, her mother remained sympathetic. And always, Del felt sure she was in Los Angeles. The solace of imagining her nearby would end, she knew, when the jam broke up. Del couldn't make herself believe that her mother was coincidentally moving to Arizona. From here on she'd be traveling alone.

Suddenly, Del felt a presence beside her.

"I could really use a biffy about now, you know?"

Del started. She turned. A petite woman in a white sundress stood at her left. In her forties, freckles, blond hair in a bun, too much lipstick on too big a smile. Her white rubber-soled shoes would have squeaked had they been on linoleum.

"A biffy?" Del's voice was suspicious, disbelieving.

"You weren't a Girl Scout?" This was an innocent question, but it registered in Del's mind as an attack.

"Actually, I was," she lied. She thought of the decorator crab. "For a little while. Back in third grade." She'd been madly envious of their uniforms at the time, especially of their badge-bearing sashes, but had felt too much an outsider to join.

"Well," said the woman, "when you go camping somewhere and you have to use an outhouse, we used to call it a biffy. Bathroom In Forest For You." She gave a tinkly laugh. "Spiders and all, what I wouldn't give." She leaned toward Del. "Or just a tree to squat behind." Another laugh. "Where's a forest when you need one? Oh, well."

Del pictured the woman as one of those insanely cheery doctor's receptionists. Then again, cheer was in short supply at the moment. "I was kinda thinking about the same thing," she said. They both turned and surveyed the freeway.

"We ought to be able to think up something. I went to Cal State Northridge. And you're at Yale, right?"

"Right." Del glanced down at her T-shirt and wondered what state Yale was in. Massachusetts? New York? She ransacked her brain while her eyes combed the rows of cars. Then she pointed.

"Hey. Way up there. Looks like an RV. Don't they have bathrooms?"

"Wow. Good thinking!" The woman grinned at Del, then patted her shoulder. The contact startled Del. "And good eyes! Let's go." The two of them set off side by side. "What a perfectly brilliant idea!"

Del hardly knew what to do with compliments. For a second, she tried on the woman as a fantasy mother—supportive, full of praise and pride in her. From what she'd seen of the world, real mothers and daughters did nothing but fight. She found herself wondering what it would actually be like to be this woman's daughter.

"You back home for the summer?" she asked Del.

"Yeah."

"What are you studying?"

Del thought. "Literature," she replied. "Nineteenth century. And chemistry." She imagined Mr. Carbon smiling. "And I'm on the swim team."

"You're certainly broad-minded."

Del had steeled herself for a different adjective—"unfocused" or "eccentric."

"They say the autumn back there's gorgeous," the woman said.

Autumn. Del tried to call up the landscapes in *Dead Poets Society.* "Yeah. It's great. The maples and the birches . . ." She suddenly ran out of tree names.

"How lucky for you. An Ivy League school. I've never lived out of California. I was born—"

"It's not like my parents are rich or something," Del interrupted. She identified with underdogs and felt uncomfortable playing a preppie. "I got a scholarship. Otherwise, forget it."

They passed a woman giving a neck massage, then a man doing push-ups against the hood of his car.

"I'm sure you're much smarter than I ever will be," the woman went on. "What high school did you go to?"

Del didn't want to say "Venice," but feared she might accidentally claim to be from the woman's home turf. She'd said she'd gone to college in Northridge. The Valley. Maybe she'd lived there before and after. "Anaheim," Del replied, putting herself in the opposite corner of L.A.

"My brother-in-law teaches at Anaheim High!" The woman turned and beamed, as if she'd just won a game-show jackpot.

Gimme a freaking break! thought Del. She struggled to smile back. Then she told herself, Chill, all high schools are the same, you can do it.

"He teaches math! Trigonometry and calculus. Mr. Beckstein."

"Yeah, sure." Then she added, "Kids really liked him." She was on thin ice—and found herself actually enjoying it. "The kind of teacher who was really, you know, really . . ."

"Young at heart," the woman supplied. "Really likes his kids. Even listens to their music."

Now Del had something to build on. She considered claiming he'd liked his students so much that he'd had an affair with a friend of hers. Del had hated her last math teacher. This punishment didn't seem to fit the crime, however, especially given her companion's sweet nature. Del sheathed her knife.

"Right. My friend Gloria had him and really liked him. Everybody thought he was cute." This was bland, but, unexpectedly, gave her a new sense of power. She could use her tongue as something other than a weapon. "We used to watch him drive off in that car he drove, I forget the—"

"A '59 Nash Rambler! A breadbox on wheels. The homeliest car you'll ever see!"

"We thought it was cool!"

"And all this time we thought he was just trying to embarrass us!" said the woman.

"And he was romantic. The way he had his wife's picture on his desk."

The woman seemed impressed. "Carl?"

Del realized she'd better cover herself. "I think it was Mr. Beckstein."

The woman smiled. "That Carl. We all love him. Everyone in my family."

Del was starting to like him herself and was wishing she could cut and paste herself into the family, then saw they'd reached the RV. It was big, barnacled with bicycles and folding chairs. They circled it, found shades covering the front window, then knocked politely at the side door. Del took note of the South Carolina license.

The door opened a crack, showing the cross section of a brunette with a sleepy toddler in her arms.

"I'm so sorry," she said softly. "I know you want a bathroom. We let everybody use it earlier, but my husband says we just can't take anyone else. The tank's full. I'm sorry." The door closed.

Del and her companion stood stunned.

"Oh, well," said the woman. "It was still a good plan. There's got to be others. And there's an exit in a mile. Want to keep walking?"

Del's bladder ached. She quickly made other plans. "Actually, I think I'll head back to my car. But thanks."

"And what was your name?"

Del could hear her calling her brother-in-law right away on her cell phone. "Elena Franco." She said it with perfect nonchalance.

"Nice meeting you."

"You, too."

The woman walked on. Del headed back the way they'd come, then turned around after two minutes, saw no sign of the woman, and marched briskly back to the RV. Audelia Thigpen had had no control over her life. Elena Franco had to pee, and she wasn't going to aim into a narrow-necked water bottle in the back seat of her car with a tarp over her.

She rolled up her hat and knocked on the RV door.

It opened. "I'm so sorry," the woman began, still holding the drowsy child. Del stuck her hat in the crack to keep the door from closing.

"I'm three months pregnant," she blurted out in a southern accent. "I know you'll understand, with your own kid and all. And I'm having some problems—I had a miscarriage last year—and I swear if I don't get to a bathroom real—"

The door opened wide.

"Thank you!" said Del. She picked up her hat, unrolled it, showed the woman the Atlanta Falcons logo. "I'm from the South, too." She put her foot on the step and climbed inside into a world of crayons and dolls and fishing gear. She followed the mother toward the rear. "My mom grew up in South Carolina," Del went on. "Wish I was back there right now. Came out here to lead a Girl Scout trip. Never a biffy around when you need one. . . ."

The freeway runs through a canyon in the Santa Monica Mountains. It rained the night before, and the air is clear and cold by L.A. standards, especially where the road's still in shadow. It's what passes for winter there—roughly equivalent to a May morning in Colorado. Twenty-seven different drivers offer impromptu prayers to the sun. Only one of them checked "Pagan" on the last census. Then it happens. The sun rises over the eastern rim and puts the entire freeway in sunshine. Two hours after that the temperature's up to fifty-eight degrees, and suddenly I hear hinges squeak. Warning chimes sound. Seat belts snap back to attention. People begin emerging from their cars in large numbers. There's stretching, bones cracking, bodies unfolding. Drivers are breaking out of their chrysalises.

The sun's touch on the skin feels motherly and personal even though it's bestowed on everyone. Drivers forget the panic inspired by immobility, take joy in the simple sensation of warmth, feel themselves wrapped in a sun-warmed towel.

They stare ahead and behind. They lean against their cars. Some do knee bends, trying to look busy. Some wonder what they're going to do for a bathroom. Their encounters with each other are clumsy. I watch them leave their private worlds and make contact with other tribes, watch them study their neighbors at close range. They're both fascinated and repelled. The wild variety within the species amazes them. They can barely believe the others are human. They're standing, chatting about traffic, while their eyes are secretly examining triple chins, hearing aids, gum-chewing jaw muscles in constant bovine motion, gigantic feet, dreadlocks, pierced eyebrows, pierced lips, pancake makeup, a wristwatch in the shape of Dali's melted clock, berets, birthmarks, bald heads, bloodshot eyes, a combined eighteen yards of tattoos of barbed-wire, scabs, scars of worrisome origin, toupees apparently bought at garage sales, age spots, pornographic earrings, fingernails chewed to the quick, lazy eyes incorrectly addressed for the past five minutes, capillaries in the nose, constellations of moles, Milky Ways of dandruff, padded shoulders, fraternity rings, the bizarre magnification of other people's glasses, hairsprayed hair, blond hair with black roots, blond hair with gray roots, blond hair with white roots, mustache hairs creeping into the mouth, gelled hair, armpit hair, nose hair, ear hair. . . . People are so incredibly strange!

Few of them have any desire to walk a mile in each other's moccasins, ditto Birkenstocks and stiletto heels, not to mention in each other's families, diets, politics, favorite colors, radio stations, definitions of fun, or creation beliefs. A lot of them retreat to their cars with relief. For others, being part of the jam unites them, gives them a temporary membership in the same club, floats them over their differences. It's a holiday. The rules have been dropped. Conversation with complete strangers is allowed. Work— that dictator—has been overthrown for the morning. The ones who stay out feel giddy, more sociable than they are, in a mood to ignore blue hair and New York Yankees caps. Some feel the release of altruism, normally doled out only to family.

Two college students turn bandanas into finger puppets, crouch low on the back seat, and improvise a show for the kids in the car behind them. A fast-talking computer programmer downloads a virus-scanning program for his neighbor's new laptop, then goes on to muck around in the BIOS resetting things—terrifying the female owner, who wants to stop him but can't find an entrance in his high-speed narration of what he's doing. He then shows her how to design her own icons, tweaks her e-mail, installs four new hot keys, dusts her desktop, and, finally, reluctantly gives the laptop back. A tow-truck driver hauling an '84 Cadillac—a dead gladiator being dragged off the arena— is asked to look at an alternator belt. He tests it with his thumb, pronounces it healthy, and then finds himself in great demand, checking car after car like a doctor making rounds, diagnosing, prescribing, comforting the relatives. For this, he's tipped with two buttermilk doughnuts, one glazed, a coupon for a free haircut, and twelve long-stemmed red roses. A woman who got a raise the day before hears on the radio that the jam won't clear till the afternoon. She stares at the bottles of water on the Culligan truck ahead of her, approaches the driver, confers, waits while he calls the office, gives him her credit card, and buys twenty-five

five-gallon containers along with a dispenser, which the driver sets up between lanes. In the course of the day, water flows into thermoses, mugs, soda cans, bottles, plastic bags, dog bowls, cookie tins, cupped hands, and open mouths.

People talk. The conversations are like chess games, all starting with the same board, then diverging. Everyone begins with the jam: expressions of disbelief, persecution, resignation. Then the road forks, usually one of three ways, toward survival tales of earlier jams, or commuting in general—allowing a smooth transition into jobs and personal information—or toward theological inquiry: What does the jam mean? The ones who go this way are like early humans trying to understand thunder. They see messages addressed personally to them in the stock market, the movement of the planets, horse-racing results, cloud shapes, and traffic tie-ups. I overhear today's jam inter-preted as a sign that the speaker is really too sick to go to work, as a punishment for a second bowl of ice cream, as a chance to review anger-management techniques, as a warning against a romantic tryst, as a sign that the brakes aren't safe, that it's time to slow down and smell the roses, that the flight to London's carrying a bomb, that it's time to get out of L.A. and move to Sedona, Big Sur, Iowa, Alaska, a houseboat in France, the Orkney Islands, the Australian outback, northern Finland, Bhutan.

People talk. Some move on to someone more inter-
esting, or more like themselves, or more beautiful. It's a
five-mile-long cocktail party composed entirely of
strangers, with no penalty for leaving one listener for
another. "So where were you going?" is the universal,
unspoken question, answered without being asked. "It's
the first day of my vacation, I'm trying to leave *L.A. . . ."*
Entire life stories are exchanged between cars. Some play
their cards close, editing their material down to a few
haiku-like lines: "I'm a copier salesman. Lost the finger
in a fireworks accident. And yourself?" Some narrate
thousand-page epics. This being L.A., some use the
screenplay form: "I'm maybe five years old, in the
kitchen, choking on a hunk of bagel. My face is blue.
Upstairs in the bedroom, my dad's asleep. Early American
décor. Back in the kitchen, I pick up the note on the counter
from my mom. It reads "Back at 5." I zoom in on the
clock on the microwave: 4:33. Then a knocking sound. I
turn and look at the back door. On the other side it's my
friend Mitzi. Short and plump, Danny DeVito in a little
girl's body and with a skate key around her neck . . ."

People gradually get used to ignoring class, race,
appearance, politics, make and model, bumper stickers.
Cell phones are loaned to those without. A black twenty-
four-year-old chalk artist works on his self-portrait on the
asphalt, giving pointers on shading, noses, eyes, and color

theory to an Italian grandmother who's just starting a Drawing Fundamentals class. Farther back, a French family on vacation becomes a center of attention. Someone asks them their impressions of Disneyland. They report they loved it. This reassures listeners that they're not Gallic snobs and lets loose a flood of questions: California wines, World War II, mistresses, real-estate prices in Provence, smelly cheeses, poor service received at a French restaurant in Redondo Beach. It's as if they're giving a press conference. Their twelve-year-old daughter is asked about French braiding. She doesn't know the term but turns out to know the skill and helps a mother braid her eight-year-old's hair. Three other women watch and carry the art back to their own cars. Each of them teaches it to two other women.

It's eleven. Then noon. The magnitude of the crash frees people to stroll, to leave their cars behind, to meet many others. I see scattered webs of community grow. Most of them are like a spider's first thread, connecting only two cars. Others are more complex. After a while, I notice that the drivers involved begin to see the life of separate cars and worlds as something strange and unnatural. It's as if the drivers have climbed up to a vista and can now look down on their former lives. A gardener from Oaxaca tells his neighbor about the time he stopped at a red light on Pico and saw a pair of hedge trimmers on the roof of the car ahead. It was a long light, so he jumped out of his truck, picked them up, knocked on the woman's window—

and the sight of a stranger holding them caused her to scream, hit the gas, shoot through the light, and get totaled by a beer truck.

"People are very afraid here," he sums up. "Of each other. And also of gardening tools."

A classics professor tells a janitor about the time he passed a car on fire on the Harbor Freeway, huge flames curling around the raised hood, a woman and child inside, a desperate man battling the fire with a floor mat while cars drove past by the hundred.

"Something's wrong with that picture," he says. "You know?"

"Something wrong with a lot of pictures," says the janitor.

The professor's mind suddenly turns toward the people injured in the crash ahead. He leaves the janitor, strides off, stops, continues on, tingling with the notion of walking all the way to the front. He has no medical training, just a will to help. He retreats to his car and debates. He's seen ambulances screaming up the empty lanes across the median. He'd probably just be in the way. It's a job for specialists. The dissertation in his briefcase calls out to be read. Then he realizes he's thinking just like the drivers who passed the car on fire—let someone else deal with it, he's too busy, not qualified. He gets out of his car and sets off for the front. He can at least offer his aid. If they turn him back, so be it.

He doesn't know that the first woman he passes walking toward him was rejected for service an hour earlier. The news on the radio that there are many injuries worked like a magnet, pulling out of the crowd forty-three volunteers offering to help. Not all are trained. One man's only connection to medicine is a stint in a hospital cafeteria. Another is an emphysema patient herself. All but five with current hospital IDs are turned back by police. At the crash site, it's noisy, chaotic, raw. There's blood on the ground, gasoline, glass. A few of the volunteers are secretly relieved to be turning around. Most wish their current jobs mattered more, wish they were making a difference to another human with a face. Wending their way back to their cars, six of them muse on changing careers.

Two miles back, a reading teacher who's used to giving hugs and pats tells a lamp store owner the tragicomedy of her smog test and doesn't even notice when she touches his forearm to underline a point. He hears nothing she says for three minutes after. His senses are overloaded with the feel of her fingers, her welcoming him into her family of touch. In nineteen years, outside of handshakes, he's never touched a customer or employee. He knows he's no hugger. What he'd forgotten is how good contact feels, especially when it's not mandatory. It's an instant banishment of solitude, an unspoken promise of mutual support. He guesses the woman's own touch circle to be vast. He sees her at the center of a thousand-spoked wheel. She's vivacious but not gabby. Her smile is a lamp that's always on, fearlessly displaying her crooked teeth. He doesn't find her particularly attractive and averts his eyes from her twelve-year-old Dodge Colt, with its ripped upholstery and molting paint. His Porsche costs more than a teacher's yearly salary. And yet he realizes he's envious. Others join, warming their hands at the fire of her smile. He doesn't want to leave her charmed circle. When newcomers enter, he's careful to keep his position at the woman's left. She laughs at a joke someone tells. In the midst of this, her right hand shoots out, rests its weight briefly on his arm again, then takes off like a bird. He stays for two and a half hours.

Del spent fifteen minutes swapping stories of the South with the woman in the RV, borrowing heavily from *To Kill a Mockingbird* and movies half-watched at the video store. The woman's toddler fell asleep in her arms while Del painted herself into long afternoons shelling peas on the porch, gave herself a doctor father and a civil rights activist mother and a grandfather who told stories of Shiloh—then realized he couldn't possibly have been alive then. She changed the topic and watched enviously as the woman laid her son down on a bed, put a pillow in place to keep him from rolling out, then turned on a tiny fan to keep him cool. His eyes were shut, his blond hair damp where his head had rested against her neck. His obliviousness to all the care he was receiving aggravated Del. She stood up. Her southern material was growing thin and her accent was beginning to stray. She thanked the woman and took her leave.

She stepped down to ground level and hadn't walked ten steps before a man with a hand-held tape recorder approached her and said, "So what were you doing on the freeway today?"

Del went instantly stiff, as if he could read her secret. She glared at him. She knew it couldn't be, and knew there was no need to tell him the truth, but felt her heart race anyway. He wore sandals and shorts and had a long, blond ponytail—clearly not a news reporter. She licked her dry lips.

"Just out for a spin," she said curtly.

"Out for a spin? At rush hour? I love it." He grinned. "So then maybe the car ads are right and there is such a thing as 'driving pleasure.' Carefree, the top down, wind whipping through your hair, while your convertible slices through the landscape"—his voice suddenly sagged—"at one-and-a-half miles an hour, surrounded by five lanes of other pleasure-mad hedonists." His eyes twinkled behind his gold wire-rims. "Out for a spin. What a concept. No offense—I've just never gotten that answer. Tell me more." He aimed the recorder toward her.

"Who the hell are you?" snapped Del.

"Whoa. Sorry." He lowered the recorder. "I'm an artist. And I'm working on a piece on road rage called "Wrong Fortune" based on how people react to getting stuck in traffic—which is similar to getting a fortune you don't like at a Chinese restaurant. 'There must be some mistake.' 'I don't deserve this.' 'No way!' So my first question is always 'Why are you here,' which is something I'd always wanted to ask anyway. You see all these zillions of other cars, you know why *you're* on the freeway, your reasons are unimpeachably sound, but what about all of *them*? Know what I mean? It's fascinating, actually, the answers."

Del's heart slowed to a canter. She looked him over. He wasn't much older than she was, probably a college student, tall and gangly, clean-shaven, wearing a black Mothers of Invention T-shirt. She liked the picture of thousands of angry drivers and one artist, fascinated rather than furious, a student of the freeway rather than its slave, immune to the raw emotions around him. She wished she could stand in his place, removed from it all, looking down. She dodged his question. "So why are they all here?"

He clicked off his recorder. "You name it. You'd think they're all going to work, but when you bother to ask you find out people are driving home to Mexico or Vermont or to study bat caves in Texas or to spread their relative's ashes in the Pacific or to get to some sale the minute the doors open, or they're going to the foot doctor or daycare or the doughnut shop or to put a baseball card in the safe-deposit box, or they're on jury duty for the trial of some guy who got flipped off by some other guy and followed him an hour till he stopped and then attacked him *and his car* with a baseball bat. Heard that one this morning."

Del leaned against the moving van behind her, taking advantage of a sliver of shade. "No kidding." Her body relaxed. "So are people going ballistic today?"

He glanced at his recorder. "The first hour I got a few classic raging lunatics. It's like being an animal control officer—you don't know how close you should get. Their philosophy, from what I can tell, seems to be that they should get everything they want and nothing they don't want."

"A weird viewpoint if I ever heard one."

"You from L.A.?"

"Atlanta." The answer came out of Del's mouth on its own, without prodding.

"I'm from Buffalo. Where the weather never gives you what you want. Here, people's expectations are too high. That's my theory, anyway. Anything inconvenient or unpleasant is an aberration, you know, instead of just the way of the world."

"Kinda like that old surfing movie," offered Del. *"Endless Summer."*

"Exactly. And people jump from that to endless happiness and endless beauty and endless life. Which would explain the whole cryonics and anti-aging thing here, don't you think?"

"And the blond wig on that seventy-year-old body." Del indicated a passing woman with her eyes.

"There's this refusal to accept anything negative. Maybe it's true all through the U.S. But I swear the fortunes in the Chinese restaurants here are *significantly* more positive than the ones I used to get in Buffalo."

"Yeah?" said Del. "What are they like there? 'You will never know happiness in this earthly realm'?"

The interviewer laughed. "Maybe not quite that grim."

"'You are a person who should not be eating four servings of sweet-and-sour pork.'"

"There you go. Realistic fortunes. News you can use."

They began strolling together. Del observed him interviewing others, impressed at how seriously he took them, watching him sincerely try to understand the man who believed traffic jams were God's punishment for our materialism. In between recording sessions they discussed freeway life: the curious absence of roadkill, the mystery of exits never taken and the possibility of lost civilizations there, why people threw cassette tapes out their windows, how someone ought to splice them together and sell a CD called *America's All-Time Most-Hated Music,* Beethoven returning to earth to find "Für Elise" used as a cell-phone ring pattern, hula dancer toys in car windows, the interviewer's own collection of plastic figures glued to the dashboard of his Dodge Dart—Jesus, Mae West, the Lone Ranger, Babe Ruth, Princess Di, dinosaurs, trolls. Several times he tape-recorded the contents of bumpers for another project he was working on: "Battered red Chevy pickup, two decals of pissing boys aiming at each other, 'This Truck Protected by Smith and Wesson,' a Marine Corps decal, one from Hussong's Cantina in Mexico, 'No on Proposition 17,' a Playboy bunny, and 'If You Enjoy Shellfish, Thank a Harvester.'"

He was studying archaeology at UCLA but seemed more passionate about his interviews and art projects, saw himself as an archaeologist of the present. He was probably among the very few thrilled by the jam. Like a pilotfish, Del stayed close but out of danger, avoiding revealing her own circumstances. She found companionship to be pleasant—a dish she'd forgotten she liked. Those drivers the interviewer recorded found him as congenial as she did. Del discovered herself feeling impatient and then possessive while he talked at length to a tank-topped twenty-something who'd stuck a row of incense sticks under her fender trim and lit them sequentially, hoping to soothe angry drivers with the scent of sandalwood. Del loathed incense and the woman's beach bunny face. After five minutes, she gave up the attempt to look interested. After ten, she drifted away from their conversation, then turned. The interviewer didn't seem to have noticed her absence.

Del spun sharply as a flamenco dancer and marched off toward her car.

 My day job's selling furniture. It's like playing house. We moved all the time when I was a kid, so naturally now I want to live in one house till I die and furnish it with huge, two-ton mahogany antiques dripping with stability and family stories. I'm seriously into furniture. I just can't afford any—so I play with someone else's. When I walk into the store and look over the floor, for me it's like a miser digging his hands into a treasure chest. More loveseats

and ottomans than you could use in ten lifetimes. But Sean, who works there with me, he sees it completely differently. For him, it's a place to meet his dream woman. Maybe two-thirds of the customers are female. They look at the furniture, he looks at them—sitting on couches, lying on beds. For him it's a preview of what it would be like living with them. He takes ten percent off for the ones he likes.

I'm thinking about him while I watch two guys meandering up the freeway. They're drain cleaners, though they actually think of that as a sideline to their real work: meeting women, preferably women in nightgowns. They were headed to a retired surgeon's house in Westwood, famous for its root-infested pipes and utter lack of females. They are not disappointed with the jam. For them, it's a golden opportunity to pursue their craft.

"I don't like being turned down," says the older one. "I want a woman who meets me to be mesmerized, not looking around the room for someone else. How do I get that? By selection!" He's twenty-eight, from Chicago, built to work in a steel mill, a foxy smile, thick black hair slicked back. I can see "Tony" stitched on his blue workshirt. "And how do I select? By analyzing information."

His partner's a new kid, nineteen, Korean descent, skinny and shy. His shirt reads "William." Got dumped by the love of his life in the cafeteria in eleventh grade, has barely spoken to a female since. It's his third day working with Tony. He feels his confidence coming back.

Tony stops. "Take that minivan there. All minivan drivers are women. So what does the car tell us about her?"

William sizes it up, shifts his weight, licks his lips. "I don't know. I guess, it's like, pretty new. . . ."

"New? Are you kidding? Don't you know cars? It's six or seven years old! And what does that tell you?"

William feels like he's back in tenth-grade Spanish with Señor McGarrity. "I guess it could, like, maybe tell you . . . "

"Maybe? Are you kidding? Open your eyes! It's a minivan! Bam, you know it's not only a woman but that she's married and has at least one kid. And it's old. Bam, her husband's not making enough to buy her an SUV like all the other mothers. Maybe lost his job, lots of conflict at home, maybe she's looking for a little fun on the side. But then your eye sees that Christian fish thing. Doesn't look good. Not that Christians don't fool around. Next, her bumper stickers. KZLA. What kind of station? Country music. All adultery, all the time. A good sign. Maybe there's hope after all. But then look next to that."

William peers at the decal. "'I Love Dachshunds.'"

"Want to know her taste in men? Check out her dog. Tiny, short legs, practically hairless. Is that me?" He grabs the hair climbing out of the neck of his shirt. "No. So I keep walking. Selection!"

They move on. William looks back at the minivan and sees a walrus-mustached man reading a martial arts *magazine in the driver's seat. He doesn't mention this to his teacher. Women are everywhere. Tony advances slowly, his senses overloaded with data. They pass on the blond whose license-plate holder reads "Zero to Bitch in 2.5 Seconds." Likewise the Nissan with the bumper sticker "God Is Coming and Is She Ever Pissed." They debate the implications of "Free Tibet." William sees an Asian beauty in his mind, skilled in rare, Himalayan sex practices. Tony's not sure if Tibet is a place or the last name of some political prisoner. He sees one of those female smarties on* Jeopardy. *They move over two lanes and turn around. Then Tony halts like a lion on the savanna, nostrils open wide, his eyes focused on a blue pickup and the brunette who's waxing it.*

"Besides dogs, the best way to know a woman's taste in men is by what they're driving. Big truck like that, eight-foot bed, she's looking for a big man. Like me." He runs his tongue over his teeth. His smile bears a slight resemblance to the grille. "Blue paint." He points at his face. "Blue eyes." He tucks in his shirt. "Observe. And learn."

William watches him saunter toward the woman. She's working on the truck's hood. He himself moves just close enough to listen.

"Like a little help?" says Tony.

The woman straightens up and wipes her brow. She's pretty, in a maroon tank top and shorts, with an athlete's build—tall, broad-shouldered.

"*Actually*—" she says. *It's hard to tell if she's going to follow this with a yes or a no. Tony butts in quickly, not taking chances.*

"It's not like I've got anything else to do. And trucks are big. I used to have this same exact truck. Ford F-350. It's a lotta work. I should know. I own my own car-detailing business. In Beverly Hills. On Olympic. South side of the street. Near Roxbury Park."

William's eyebrows shoot up involuntarily at this lie. He's impressed to see his teacher put into practice two of his precepts at once: "Make as many connections with the woman as you can," and "Confuse the woman with too much information." Her hair's short and wet with sweat. She reminds William of his high-school sweetheart. He sees a movie clip in his head in which Oliver Hardy turns and says, "And this is my associate, Mr. Laurel," but Tony makes no such move.

"Actually," *the woman says,* "I don't need any help."

Tony ignores this. "I did Danny DeVito's Rolls last week."

William recognizes Precept Number Seven: "Don't fear to tell lies that can't be disproved."

"No kidding," *says the woman.*

"Got one of Mel Gibson's Ferraris there right now."

The woman doesn't seem impressed. She drinks from her water and examines Tony with a curious squint, as if he were a two-headed chicken.

"I do work at customers' houses, too. If you ever want anything done. Stripes, rustproofing—"

William recognizes the attempt to get her address.

"Thanks," says the woman. Her voice is flat. She goes back to buffing the hood.

"Or I could put you on our e-mail list so you could find out when we're having a special, if you want."

William mentally checks off "Attempt to get woman's e-mail address."

"Actually, I don't want," says the woman. She moves around the truck and disappears from sight, working on the rear fender. William watches his teacher rack his brains.

"Arnold Schwarzenegger liked my work so much on his Jags that he invited me to play golf with him last week."

No answer from the woman. The truck shakes slightly from the force of her buffing.

"He's on a film right now. Said he might need some extras in a couple of weeks."

No answer. Tony feels like he's an actor in an empty theater. "If you're interested," he adds.

No response. He wants to call it quits but doesn't want to fail in front of his student.

"Action film. Alien invasion. They're gonna be shooting in Griffith Park, I think. Over by the golf course."

No answer. The truck shakes harder. William, who's terrified of rejection, groans inside.

"You play golf at all yourself?" Tony asks.

No answer. The words hang in the air as if spoken into the Grand Canyon. Tony exhales. He wipes the sweat off his forehead. He looks back at William and shrugs his shoulders.

"Nice talkin' to you." His voice has a bitter edge. He calls William forward with an angry motion of the arm. They stalk off in silence. William turns. On the truck's rear bumper is a sticker reading "This Is Not My Boyfriend's Truck." Next to that is a Gay Pride Parade decal. He decides not to bring it up.

 Del's stomach was growling like a caged beast. She'd skipped breakfast out of nervousness and hadn't eaten anything other than eight Oreos two hours before. She looked at her watch. It was almost one o'clock. After leaving the interviewer, she'd returned to her car, read a long time, gotten tired of being cooped up, and was now drifting aimlessly down the shoulder. She scented food on the wind. It was coming from her left. She stopped near a pair of men in suits, all three of them focused on the same smell.

"It's down there somewhere," said the gray-haired one.

Del looked out over the guardrail. A self-storage lot, a tool-rental business covered with a thick vine of graffiti, shabby apartment buildings, all below the level of the freeway. The men seemed to be studying a sign reading "Carnicería La Reina."

"*Carne* means 'meat,'" said the younger one. "Like chili con carne."

The gray-haired man nodded. "So what've we got? 'Rain of meat'?"

"Doesn't *reina* mean 'queen'?"

"Don't ask me. I don't care where it came from—a queen, a king, a horse. I was on my way to *breakfast!*"

Del spotted two dark-skinned men walking into the shop.

"You suppose the natives are friendly?" asked the gray-haired man.

The other one considered. "Probably." He shaded his eyes with his hand. "We could get in and out pretty quick. You got cash?"

Del loathed their tone—wary explorers paddling upstream into darkest L.A., making sure they'd packed enough trade beads. She knew they had to be starved to consider going down the steep embankment in their shiny loafers, then to hack a trail through ivy and bushes and get over a chain-link fence. It was more trouble than she was interested in, even though she'd lived in Spanish-speaking neighborhoods and used to buy hot sandwiches at a *carnicería* near her house. She thought about misinforming them in her best Chicana accent that *carnicería* meant "car dealer," then decided to move on.

Unlike the others on the freeway, she had a month's worth of food in her car. This self-sufficiency pleased her. And yet, she wasn't about to fire up her camp stove. She also found herself reluctant to bite into the first of an endless series of peanut-butter sandwiches. She stopped, thought she tasted a new food scent with her nose. She saw a line of people. Then she made out the lunchwagon, the kind she'd seen at construction sites, the kind Opal called "roach coaches" and had warned her never to eat from. Del knew she needed to save money. But surely, she reasoned, she deserved a reward for pulling off her escape. She sped up her gait and took her place in line.

The lunchwagon was ancient, a freeway warrior covered with scars and scrapes. The Hispanic cashier and cook inside were frantically trying to meet demand. Del heard a man in a seersucker suit at the head of the line order two hot dogs.

"We don't got no more hot dogs," the cashier shot back.

"Hamburgers, then. Lettuce, tomatoes, *no onion—*"

"No more hamburgers. Just what's on the sign."

"*What* sign?"

The cook stuck a greaseboard out the window and hung it on a hook. Del could see that it had been much erased.

"Six dollars for *one taco?*" yelled the customer. "Are you crazy?"

"It was *three* when my wife was here," someone called out.

"You a businessman, right? Company that makes biggest profit is the best, right? Your prices go up and down. Our prices, too. Today lucky day. Prices up. What's your order?"

The man stormed off, swearing. Others paid without protest. The list of offerings shrank dramatically while Del waited. When the Russian woman who ordered the last burrito refused to pay ten dollars, the cashier, in a stroke of entrepreneurial genius, auctioned it off, pitting two well-heeled bidders against each other and finally getting thirty-five dollars, to the entertainment of the crowd. The Russian woman vowed to report the cashier. By the time Del reached the front, they were sold out of everything but pinto beans, white bread, and Life Savers. She ordered a cup of pintos and a roll of Life Savers, couldn't talk the cashier lower than three dollars, scowled, then opened the roll of candy and called out in full voice, "What do I hear for this cherry Life Saver?" She held it up over her head. "We'll start the bidding at a dollar!" There was laughter. "Or, if you're on a budget, you can come up and just lick it." More laughter. "At ten cents a lick." Laughter and boos, directed at the cashier. Del threw him a glance, then left, a local hero. She sat on the guardrail, spooning the steaming beans into her mouth. It made no sense, given the hot weather and her bankroll—now down to $131. Don't worry, be happy, she told herself. It's a celebration. Enjoy it.

She finished and strolled back toward her car, passing through rock music, reggae, easy listening, and talk radio, all issuing from boom boxes, each listener fighting to drown out his neighbors. The war of all against all. That was L.A., Del reflected, even when traffic was stopped. In the jam, music served as a fortress wall, keeping foreignness out and familiarity in.

A newspaper page blowing in the breeze pressed against her leg. Del picked it up—and there was the Jumble, the mixed-up word puzzle she used to tackle back in grammar school. She'd been proud of her early reading, felt grown up reading the newspaper, thought her speed at solving the Jumble would make her more adoptable. Del smirked at it, walked on, then turned the page over. Wedding photos. It struck her suddenly that she didn't have family pictures like other people. No albums. No photos in her wallet. She had a few school yearbooks, but they'd been left behind. The one foster family she'd liked, whose photo she wouldn't have minded having, had never seemed to take pictures.

She reached her car and climbed into the back. It was stifling inside—and at once her mind went back to that family, to her first day there, to standing between the white curtain and the sunny window, hiding away in that world of warmth. She was four or five. Her foster mother must have seen her shoes. Del remembered her asking, "You want to stay there a while?" Del had nodded her head. She must have seen that, too. "That's just fine. I'm glad you like it there." The next time she'd stepped inside the curtain, her foster mother had put a tiny stuffed dog on the window sill for her to play with. Then a toy car. Then a family of wooden mice.

Del rolled down the windows and lay down in the back. She looked at the wedding photos in the newspaper, then idly read the announcements. Without a father, who would give her away at her wedding, if she ever got married? He already gave you away, dummy, she answered herself. Both of 'em did. "The bride is the daughter of Charles and Janine

Whitcomb of Grenada Hills. . . ." Definitely no announcement for me, Del thought. It would be one big blank. She remembered one of her social workers talking to her foster mother: "They always head for their natural parents when they run away. These kids run away *to* home." She'd been twelve then. She'd wished she'd had that option. Del felt the sadness again now, moving in like a tide. She tried reversing it, reminded herself that having no photos or connections made it easier to cut free. L.A. had no gravity pulling on her. A jailhouse with the door left open. This was all true. She tried to avoid thinking about how good it would feel to hear someone she cared about calling her back.

 Northbound, just past the crest. Middle lane. A delivery truck for Southland Auto Parts. The driver's black, forty-eight, a baritone in his church choir in Inglewood. There's a briefcase on the floor, not for pens and papers but cassettes: The Mighty Clouds of Joy, Mahalia Jackson, Blind Boys of Alabama, the Dixie Hummingbirds. It's been hours since he turned the music off to save his battery. He looks out, perched higher than the cars, his mind idling. A bulldog hood ornament catches his eye. He finds

himself thinking about a beagle he used to own. Then his mind pivots to the stray dog he saw the day before, downtown on Spring Street, some kind of mutt, tail down, glancing over its shoulder while it trotted, that lost look in its face. "Sometimes I Feel Like a Motherless Child" begins playing in his head. He hums along, then begins singing. All at once he's back in Tennessee, five years old, leaving his mother's funeral, walking out of the wooden church, his aunt holding one hand, his uncle the other, no hand left for the tears, turning right instead of left at the street, heading toward their old Studebaker, knowing he'd never see his home again.

He comes to the third verse. "Motherless children have such a hard time. . . ."

He calls up the faces of his aunt and uncle. They were older. Didn't seem to like children. Rules and commandments, but never a smile. It was his aunt who was his blood relation. His uncle called him "the boy" or "him." Locked him in the pig barn when he wet the bed. They were at the opposite end of the state from where he'd lived before, far to the east, in the Smokies. He'd never seen mountains before. He took to exploring. He liked the woods better than being with his aunt and uncle. Began sleeping out for a night. Then two or three. The summer he was fifteen, he put what he owned in a grain sack, walked into the trees, and never went back. It was harder living off the land than he'd thought it would be. Frost came early at that altitude. He got tired of being hungry, then of being cold. He walked all the way to Asheville, cleaned bathrooms in a fleabag hotel in exchange for a room without heat, then hitchhiked out to California, where he stayed. He knew his uncle wouldn't have missed him, but years later he felt sure that his aunt must have worried. He'd never written. By now, she must be dead. He'd always wondered if she'd tried to find him.

"Sometimes I feel like freedom is near. . . ."

He sings the last three verses, ignoring the woman to his left eyeing him over her Entertainment Weekly. *He's got plenty of time. He doesn't skip any verses. The tune's strong, sad, soothing, a dark lullaby, a river listened to at night. He makes his way down to the last line, "So far Mama from you, so far"—and stops midway. He sits up straight. He realizes he had the dream again last night. This time it was on the Pasadena Freeway. Traffic was stopped in both directions. And there, in a car pointed the other way, was his mother. He scrambled out of his car, jumped over the median, ran up to her. Her window glass went suddenly opaque. He could just make out her head. He called her name. He kissed the glass. The car was covered with dust and leaves. "You been driving around here, same as me?" he asked her. The head shape gave a nod. "Have you been watching me all along?" The head nodded again. He squeezed his face up against the glass. "Why'd you go and die?" he cried out. Then her lane began moving. He had to trot to keep up. Then he was running, then sprinting. Her window opened a crack. Then he heard her voice. "Had to leave, sugar-bee." Her old name for him. "No choice. Just like now." And he lost his grip on the door handle and her car raced off, oak leaves flying in his face. He stopped. He picked up one of the leaves—and saw, just before he awoke, that it was the same kind he remembered from the oaks in Tennessee.*

 Del finished off her water, climbed outside, and discreetly opened the trunk partway. She had visions of a mob of thirst-crazed drivers storming her car for her two dozen bottles. No way I'm sharing these, she vowed. She grabbed one and quickly closed the trunk. Hot car roofs seemed to melt the air and set it writhing. She settled back inside, put Lassie on her lap, and propped *Les Misérables* against him. She read for another hour, then tried the radio. Traffic wasn't expected to start moving before four. Was this intentional? A chance for her to reconsider? If there's a God, Del thought, and that's what he's doing, he was definitely wasting his time—and a lot of other people's. She couldn't bear being stuck any longer, grabbed her water, got out, and started walking.

She recognized her neighbors by now: the Japanese-looking man from the Lexus, the smoker from the black Mercedes, the three women on vacation from Wisconsin who should have been complaining the loudest but instead had been merrily talking non-stop with each other and anyone who passed. Sun-stroke victims, Del concluded. She gave the garbage truck a wide berth and for lack of something better to do gradually eased into the slightly bowlegged walk of a motorcyclist who passed her. She slipped into his life—a sore butt, hearing shot, sweat flowing underneath his black leather. She didn't fancy this as a vacation destination and ditched him in favor of a surfer type. She was sure no one around her noticed, or would care even if they had. They were all strangers, camped briefly on a road— a place without any memory. There were no crosses and flowers here marking deaths. Anything done here vanished like skywriting.

Del moved her shoulders and head down slightly, crawling into the surfer's frame, tried for his slightly stoned expression. Don't worry, be happy. This was what she needed. She got into it, felt better, wandered over to the median. The empty lanes beyond were eerily quiet, allowing her to overhear a man on a phone describing his job-hunting problems. He was two months behind on rent, had been promised retraining, would lose his car if he couldn't make the next payment. His talk made Del anxious. For the first time, she wondered what she would do if her plans didn't pan out, if she couldn't find work, if she actually ran out of money for food. She turned and strode off to escape the thought. Then her ears picked up the sound of someone singing.

She passed a gasoline tanker, then a Corvette with a For Sale sign in the window, then rounded an old pickup and came on a red-faced man singing a ballad to a dozen spectators seated on the guardrail. There was an English lilt to his voice. He sang unaccompanied and made instruments seem unneeded as he unrolled the tale of a shipwreck off Australia. The crowd applauded when he finished. Del thought he'd sing another, then saw a skinny man stand, look around, and say, "Well, who's next?"

There was a pause. It seemed to be an impromptu talent show. "Don't hide your light under a bushel," the man said. "Bushel might catch on fire." Another pause. "And remember, if no one steps up, I'll get my banjo back out of its case."

"No, not again!" called a tortured voice.

Del took a seat on the rail. A woman three spots down got up, stood between cars where the singer had, cleared loose gravel away, then got the crowd clapping and put on a clogging demonstration to the beat. Del put down her water and clapped with the rest. She'd never seen anything like that before. Appalachian tap dancing, the woman called it. Next, a man juggled oranges, then road flares instead of clubs, then two flares and a tire iron. The crowd grew. An earnest woman with a guitar played a song she'd written. A UPS driver played "Baby, You Can Drive My Car" on a kazoo. A long, unfunny joke was told. A man in a Hawaiian shirt mumbled incoherently while performing an endless drum solo on a hubcap held between his knees. The woman beside Del punched her cell phone. Interest was fading. No one claimed the stage after the drummer. Not exactly a hard act to follow, thought Del. Suddenly, she found herself standing and walking to the front.

"Cell phone calls overheard today," she announced. The woman who'd been dialing next to her snapped hers shut. The crowd looked expectantly up at Del. She reached into her pocket, pulled out an imaginary phone, and flipped it open. "Eight-fifty A.M. A Mercedes driver." A hiss from the crowd. She thought of the man in the black Mercedes near her Datsun, strolled in front of the guardrail, phone to ear, then stopped. "Ah, at last." An upper-class accent. "I just purchased one of your Z-Class vehicles. With the Z-Class lifetime warranty program. And I'm sorry to say, it's already happened." A pause. "This morning." She mimed flipping through a booklet. "Ah, here it is." A reading voice. "Furthermore, owners of the Z-Class Mercedes shall enjoy free roadside service, loaner car privileges, free croissants in the service waiting room, free raspberry preserves,"—no laugh at this—"and for forty-eight months will not suffer from annoying coworkers, the common cold, disappointment in love—" A chuckle. "Disappointment in the stock market. Rain on owner's birthday." She racked her brains. "Rain during owner's children's soccer games. Taxes." She saw her ending. "Death—unless desired by owner." A decent laugh. "Or traffic jams!"

She'd given her punch line too early, while they were still laughing. She flipped the phone shut. They must have heard the line. The applause was modest. It had been fun. She looked at her empty place on the guardrail. She'd only been up there for a minute. Then she remembered the surfer, turned her hat around, leaned up against a car, and flipped open the phone.

"Eleven forty-one. Red Mazda pickup with surfboard." Plodding, clueless voice, an octave lower than normal. "Yeah. I'd like to order a pizza." A laugh at the impossibility of delivery. "Yeah. Pepperoni. And pineapple." Her own favorites. "And chocolate chips." A groan. "Excellent. . . . And peanut butter . . . and salsa and chips . . . and vitamin C . . . and Clearasil.

. . . Just put *everything* on it, man." Time to think while they laughed. "Where am I? You know the freeways, man? Excellent. Write this down, man. I'm on the Santa Monica. And I'm like the two thousandth . . . eight hundredth . . . sixty-fifth car *east* of the San Diego turnoff, man." A big laugh. This time she waited for it to end but found she was out of material. "Red Mazda pickup. You can't miss it. Excellent!" She pocketed the phone.

More applause this time. The crowd had grown slightly. Del didn't want to get off the wave. Someone called out, "Do another one!" She tried to think. She needed a female, for contrast. She scanned the crowd, found her gaze snared by a redhead, flashed on Shirley MacLaine, then past lives—and flipped the phone back open.

"Twelve thirty. Honda Accord." She reached for her seventh foster mother's New York accent. "Darva? It's me. Norma Fishburn." Her old computer teacher, the only name that came to mind. "I know I just started the channeling class, and I haven't gotten in touch with my past lives yet, but I'm in a traffic jam, a real doozy, and I'm having claustrophobia like you wouldn't believe, so what I was wondering, and I'll pay you, I promise, on my mother's marble gravestone"—one of Opal's favorite phrases—"what I need is for you to get me out of here *and into somebody else right now!"* A laugh. "One of *your* past lives, if you're not using it, you know. Someone old, from before there were cars. I was thinking maybe you could put me in an ancient Egyptian, just for today. If you've got one free." Chuckles. Del paused while her character listened. "Booked through the weekend. No kidding." Del thought ahead while miming listening. "A Phoenician slave? Hmmm. I don't know. Do they eat fish? 'Cause I don't eat fish." One of Opal's traits. "Except tuna. Did they have tuna salad back then?" A dead end. She paused. "And what kind of slave? Cause I don't do windows." A laugh. "And no mopping, either." A pause. "Light housework? You're positive?" She saw her ending. "All right, I'll take it. So when do we switch? *And make sure she knows how to drive a manual!"*

Her biggest laugh. She snapped the phone shut to applause. Someone whistled. A middle-aged man caught her eye. Face black as obsidian, a red beret on his head, a gold lower tooth glinting in the sun. His laughter, she could tell, was genuine, his smile giving off light like a star. Their eyes met briefly, completing the electrical circuit. It struck her as miraculous that she, over here, had caused him, over there, to laugh. She wanted to do it again. An idea came: a car salesman roaming the lanes, buying up cars with For Sale signs and selling them to other drivers. A chance to get back at the guy who'd sold her the Datsun. She closed her eyes for ten seconds to think and get in character. When she opened them, the crowd was on its feet.

"What's happening?" she asked.

She heard an engine start in the distance. "Someone said they're gonna start letting us move pretty soon," said the banjo player. "The far right lane, anyway."

The crowd sorted itself into different directions.

"Hey, you were great," he added.

Del's mind was on driving, her salesman skit forgotten. "Thanks." She was one lane from the far right. Surely her lane would be next. She started back, then remembered her water bottle and U-turned. It was there below her spot on the guardrail. She bent to pick it up, and stared. Underneath it was a folded five-dollar bill. She squinted, wondering if she was seeing things. She pulled out the bill and opened it. Lincoln's gentle eyes peered into her own. She was astounded that someone had left it for her. It was the sun rising in the west, an impossible event, utterly contrary to her theory of human nature. She stood and looked about, wondering who it was. She saw only backs, heading toward cars. There was no way to know. It would always be a mystery.

She made her way back toward her car. In her pocket, she could feel the five-dollar bill. In her right hand, she carried her water bottle. In her mind, she carried the picture of the black man's gold-toothed smile. Even secondhand, in memory, it made her grin. It was the first photograph from her new life. She imagined a white mat and gold frame around it.

Her mantelpiece was bare.

She set it in the center.

And then, suddenly, information speeds down the freeway's spinal column. The eighteen-wheeler has been moved. The last of the crumpled cars have been towed. The northbound lanes will open one at a time. The southbound lanes will clear in half an hour.

This news cuts conversations like scissors. Cell phones snap shut by the hundreds. People scurry back to their cars as if the film of the afternoon is being run in reverse. A French-braiding lesson is briskly wrapped up; games of cribbage and poker dissolve. An Ethiopian taxi driver who's been enduring a Hollywood podiatrist's life story faces front again, closes the window between them, guns his Plymouth, and rests his hand expectantly on the meter. I see waving. A few phone numbers are exchanged. There's jubilation. I also hear regret. The temporary vil-

lage, like a fair, is taken down. I watch an Irish fiddler playing "Paddy on the Turnpike" at an unplugged, unplanned talent show that's taking place on a big flatbed truck. He sees his audience scatter, finally stops, and jokes, "Am I out of tune, then?" My car is nearby. I see the fiddler's cap on the ground. I fly low and drop five dollars in it. Then I float down, somersault in slow motion, and reenter my car, feet first, through the sunroof.

I touch down and collect myself. I put my hands on the steering wheel. It feels strangely solid. I look around. I must be visible again. The woman on my right gives me the thumbs-up. I notice I've lost the power to hear her thoughts.

It turns out we still have a while to wait. My own thoughts turn practical. Catching a different flight. My daughter. Our latest dog, another stray from the pound. We're not moving, but my mind's already looking ahead. I miss looking down, miss that astronaut's vantage point. I take my eyes off the windshield and glance in the rearview mirror instead. There, behind me, is the French horn player. He's sitting in his Cadillac's back seat. He's strung a string from side to side, probably tied to the coat hooks, and hung pages of music to it with clothespins. He's practicing. It's classical music. He's got a gray beard, a bushy one, and I'm wondering how he keeps the hairs out of his mouthpiece—when suddenly, from nowhere, Sartre's line comes into my head: "Hell is other people."

And then, like those nested wooden dolls, that thought opens up, and a new one pops out: L.A. is a vast, ludicrous, lethal, infuriating collection of Other People. I remember flying high above the road's crest, with a view of both the Valley and downtown, from the beach all the way to the mountains—an immense, gray, writhing battlefield of crossed wills.

And then, within that, another thought: Other People are all we've got.

The thought rings in my head. The woman who'd been plucking her eyebrows on my left. The guy with the bald spot shaped like Montana. The French horn player. The other drivers. They're all we have to connect to. And without connection, we can't survive. Trust me—I tried it once. I think of all the people I saw in the jam. They're all so strange. We're all so strange. I am one of the Other People.

And then, within that, a further, final thought: It's not just other people we have to accept. It's Otherness. Things we have no control over, didn't ask for, don't deserve. History. Earthquakes. Cancer. Family. Traffic jams. "It is what it is."

I'm blinded. Dazed. I get a glimpse of acceptance, like a mountain peak guarded by clouds. And suddenly I know that's where I want to go. That I've got to go. That I've been waiting to leave.

I've been on that path a year now, and I have to tell you I don't feel that much closer. It's a lifetime trek, a destination you never reach. Anger comes so much more easily than acceptance. Dragging an eighteen-wheeler off the road is easier than open-hearted acceptance. The jam was just a beginner's exercise in giving up control, in receiving with good grace everything given us at birth and everything that comes after. In eating everything on our plates.

I hear celebratory honking ahead. In the car behind me, the man has hauled his French horn up to the front seat. The car's gotta be an automatic. I try not to think about how he steers. I start my engine. Then the car ahead creeps forward. I take off the brake and shift into Drive. I'm moving. It feels surreal to see the landscape passing by on its own. My mind drifts. I see myself landing in Boulder, describing the jam to my cab driver, hugging my daughter, smelling her hair. When I was pregnant, I was under the illusion that I'd be getting unconditional love, not giving it. Those first few years were so much tougher than I'd imagined. She's been more than I could accept at times. Plenty of traits I didn't order. If your kids had colic, you know what I mean. A picky, stubborn eater—same as I was. Unending practice in giving up control. But I feel a glow coming from my right. My satchel's there. Inside it, my wallet. And inside that, five different photos of her. She's my precious Other Person. I can't wait to see her.

From behind me, I hear the French horn. I've never been much for classical music. I lower all the windows to let it in.

THE END